Crooked Halo

Kay Dockhorn

ISBN: 0994394411
ISBN-13: 978-0994394415

DEDICATION

Dedicated to every girl in any type of relationship.

CONTENTS

ACKNOWLEDGMENTS

I'd like to thank my family and especially my younger brother for their continual support, and a special thanks to my best friend Ashleigh Shankar for always being there for me and helping me through a lot of my writers block when it came up

PROLOGUE

I hear the baying of the angel-hunters much closer than before.

'Don't they ever give up?' I think angrily.

Around me autumn has just set in.

The leaves are coloured bright red, orange and yellow, drifting aimlessly towards the ground.

A gentle breeze catches my hair leading them further in my direction. My feet slap the ground hard.

If my wings hadn't been tied up I would've flown away so that they'd lose my scent, but they were too smart for that kind of trickery anyway. Melody flew above me, warning me of the obstacles ahead. Melody is my bonded Angel-Animal;

they choose us when we advance to 2nd year training.

Melody is a teenage horse with a brilliant white coat flecked with honey tones on her back and legs.

Her forehead has a swirl splashed with shining silver and dotted with sparkling gold infused into her fur.

Her mane is cream coloured with streaks of hidden turquoise showing in both it and her tail.

Her eyes are a hazel brown and her wings are stark white with streaks of star silver and flecks of gold near the tips of the feathers.

Without her I wouldn't have been able to escape that torturous place.

She flew me over the poisoned wall, safely.

That wall is where most met their end, like Lily...

'I still can't believe they let her die!' I think angrily, tripping over a log.

Looks like I was drifting into one of my future visions again. Most people would think that it was good to have special powers and believe me they do come in handy… but it's rather irritating that I can't stay conscious during the whole process of receiving information about the future in the present.

Oh great, just what I need, one of the hounds has caught up to us. He keeps yapping excitedly to tell his pack and master where I am.

Suddenly I have this crazy idea, so of course I attempt it. Slowing my pace. the hound catches up very quickly and tries to pin me down. Using his teeth as scissors, I cut through the ropes that bind my wings in place and takeoff.

It feels amazing to be able to stretch them again.

Calling 'Melody!' in my head we both fly west into the sunset, and towards the Humans Forest.

I know it doesn't sound scary, but humans always try to destroy things that are unknown to them, like, for example,

Angels-in-Training. Which is why we normally steer clear of them completely.

As the moon starts to open its white eye I know we're in danger of being fired at, but if we stop now, the hounds are bound to find us.

They never enter the Humans Forest because they fear being captured by them and made pets for the rest of their lives. If we can make it to the edge of the forest we will be much safer than we are now.

As we fly through the trees I find a suitable place to rest and set about finding some food for Melody and myself.

Melody thinks, 'Be careful, Myrelle.' sending her thoughts my way before landing in the tree, on one of the thicker branches, and resting her tired wings.

I give her a faint acknowledgment and return an hour later with grass from the Honey-dew Plain

and some berries from Strawberry Fields.

I sit in the crook of a branch next to the tree's trunk and look

longingly at the stars.

'Finally, a chance to see the stars without having to peek through a wired net for a roof.'

I think to myself, the hint of a smile playing over my lips,

And only now do I allow myself to truly believe that I've made it out of there.

Once we've eaten our fill I curl up in the crook of that tree and allow my eyes to drift shut.

I fall asleep quickly, and that's when it happened, the Dreaming began...

CHAPTER 1 : MYRELLE, 1 WEEK LATER - THE MEAN AND THE MERCIFUL

That dream still hasn't gone away. I was flying over the Humans Forest very near the edge of the Human World with Melody.

I spotted a camp fire very isolated from society and wanted to investigate when I found myself falling through the air, a blanket covering my wings and a net holding it in place. Melody didn't seem to be of concern to them because she just flew behind me, never leaving my side for more then an hour at a time, and never being further away from me than necessary.

This dream has stayed with me much longer than any other ever has and it seems to be of great importance.

I heard that girls voice again. She kept telling me to

"trust them."

I wish she could be more specific.

I know her name now, she said to call her Misty,

and she looked to be a few years younger than me and is

definitely Angel-Type.

For some reason her voice seems familiar to me although I don't know where I've heard it before.

"Ouch!" I exclaimed loudly.

I'd just flown into a rather thick tree branch;

just shows how much I need to work on my focus.

My Angel instructor always said that a sun and water crossed Angel never has a good focus level even though they have the ability to control water, sunlight and heat naturally. I'm special though because I'm the Princess of Angel Haven, the largest city of Angels. I can't tell anyone though, or else they'll find me again, and drag me back to that place.

It's even worse than the Institution so I have to be careful.

As best I can tell I'm able to control water, sunlight and heat, but I can also see the future and make objects invisible.

I'm still working on mastering the invisibility thing though. My angel instructor also said that a Prince or Princess would gain a new power every autumn when the blue moon shines, for 5 years, of which two have already passed.

In 2 weeks time I will go to the shining pool and be faced with an impossible decision or a horrible truth that will determine my next power during a blue moon.

My instructor informed me that spirit would play an important part in my next power.

I've been flying for hours now, patrolling the skies for even the slightest hint of smoke from a fire, or specks in the air that could mean Angel Hunters are in the area, looking for me.

I'm really tired now.

Melody says, 'Get some rest Myrelle, you'll need your strength tomorrow.' Surprised by her voice of authority and intrusion into my mind I do as she suggests.

As soon as I land I collapse in the crook of a tree and fall asleep.

Melody keeps her guard up with one ear pricked for noise before snoozing lightly under the protection of thousands of stars.

Melody wakes up during the night, but I can't be bothered to get up, so I just let her be.

~

I catch the scent of wood that burns, and birds that cry shrilly while trying to save their hatchlings and nests to no avail.

The growl of a tiger directs my attention to the center of the fray.

Two tiger, cubs one red, one white, are held up in a net while men jeer wildly at the tigress who cannot reach her children without being shot dead, stabbed or struck with a wooden pole.

Sighing heavily, I fly down to the men blasting them with gusts of wind from my wings until they drop the net of cubs and flee for the nearby village, probably hoping to catch and sell me.

'Good luck.' I think sourly. The cubs mother gave me a kind expression of gratitude for helping her before returning to the forest, melting into the surrounding trees as though she'd never even set foot in that clearing.

After that I flew back to the tree where Myrelle slept and went to sleep for good.

~

I wake up at dawn startled out of sleep by the starling's call. The sun rises in the east casting everything into an eerie light;

only after enjoying the sunrise do I smell the burnt wood that Melody picked up on the night before.

Looking down, I gaze at a horror scene. Kilometres of trees are charred and blackened from the forest fire in the west.

A few trees from us the fire was extinguished by a powerful water source.

Smoke darkens the sky and soon reaches us.

As if waking from a dream it starts to rain and the smouldering embers are quenched.

Glancing at Melody for an explanation, she states, 'I couldn't direct them into the forest now, could I? They were probably hoping to smoke out some rare animals, tigers for example.'

At that moment all the distorted sounds in my head made sense; the shrill birdcalls, the roaring predators, and fearful yelps of dogs. Whatever my vision had been about, it was going to happen, soon.

Unsurprisingly Melody didn't seem concerned in the least while I was the one fretting over how to alter my vision, because you cannot stop the future, you can only change it.

Much as I think about it though I cannot, for the life of me, figure out how to avoid getting caught again. The rain pouring around me suddenly feels warm compared to the chilling feeling of hopelessness that's slowly trying to creep into me. I'd seen it in so many eyes so many times before, but only now was I starting to understand why they'd felt that way.

There was no escape from what was to come. For them, it had been witnessing and then experiencing one painful death after the other, but I'd have to wait and see what the future had in store for me.

CHAPTER 2 : RICK - CAMPING OUT

The rain has been going on for hours.

I'm surprised that Rose hasn't complained to me yet.

We're much closer to the Angel Plains than I'd like and the animals keep telling Rose that a great change will occur soon. Yes, I did say, tell Rose. Since Rose developed her first and only power that allows her to communicate with animals she is a lot more withdrawn than a normal kid would be.

We are both Angels, but I'm secretly an Angel Tracker. Rose was supposed to be an Angel-in-training a year ago but I didn't sign her up. I didn't want to lose our only hope to redeem our family.

Rose is the only Angel in our family who is pure; she's never done anything bad in her life and always makes good decisions.

Although I'm starting to doubt that it was such a good
decision on her part to go camping this weekend,
but she just keeps saying, "Don't worry about it, Rick,
It'll all be worth it."
Not to say I don't trust my little sis, but if this isn't worth it she'll have
to deal with our parents,
not me.

At least we brought the water resistant tent.

"Damn!" I swear quietly. I just got a text from HQ.

"Angel has escaped, if you see it, capture it and bring it back." Well, if there were a time and a place that said, Duty Calls
any better than this one, it'd have to be pretty damn good.

Of course there are always setbacks in an important situation, so of course it stops raining five minutes later and Sarah steps out of the forest followed bravely by her two loyal cubs. Rose rushes out to greet them as soon as they appear, but then something changes, and I know this isn't just a friendly visit.

Rose looks at Sarah and her eyes slowly widen in disbelief as the tigress tells her story and then they disappear back into the forest.

Rose whispers something inaudible and then says,

"I don't believe it! She saw a bonded Angel Alacorn!"

As soon as I hear the word bonded, my ears prick up.

"Did you just say Bonded Angel Alacorn?" I ask carefully.

"Yes I did," she snaps back in angry retort.

I whistle softly and mutter something to her about going to collect some firewood.

No sooner am I out of sight I stretch my wings and soar though the treetops to the nearest clearing. There, I hustle up the pack and they pick up the scent.

They begin to whimper softly as the smoke mingles with the trail, but the estimated angle of travel has already been set

and they begin their pursuit.

It's amazing that an animal can sense an Angel's presence and we can't, even though we have two times more sensitive senses than an ordinary human.

They suddenly start yapping excitingly and bolting towards a near clearing.

A sharp, low whistle brings them to a stand still as I order them back to their hidden posts.

Annoyed but obedient, they retreat from their prize and allow me to catch a glimpse of the angel animal I was seeking,

My breath caught in my throat as I beheld the Alacorn mare, my eye immediately caught onto her silver and gold flecks and a flash of turquoise drew my attention to her head where I see the metallic colouring of a sign of royalty. No-one knows why some royals have a golden mark while others have a silver one, that's just the way it is.

Most royal bonded animals are tied with other royals though there are some rare occasions where the royal animal bonds with a normal commoner.

In my own way I am respectful of this angel who's managed to escape with only their bonded animal friend.

Sending a quick message to Storm, I settled down in a tree where I could observe the Alacorn without her seeing me.

As Storm landed I beheld my bonded Pegasus.

He's pitch black with a mane and tail of dark brown, highlighted with cherry red and silver streaks like an angry storm. He had flecks of silvery white across his back and legs with a single honey coloured sock on his left foreleg.

He looked at me expectantly, but then something changes in him, he seems to tense up even more than usual,

and his eyes widen in shock and disbelief.

He whispered mentally, 'Do you know who she is?!'

He was really mad at me, but I still didn't know why.

'No…' I think, my thoughts transferred to Storm through our mental link.

In answer he quietly thought her title in full, 'She is Melody Songstress, bonded to the unknown and is the daughter of the King of Unicorns and Queen of Pegasus. She has the wings of a Pegasus and the powers of a Unicorn without having to carry her horn.'

I honestly couldn't believe what I'd just heard, 'That would explain the mark of royalty on her forehead… but what do you mean by bonded to the unknown?' I asked, confused.

In answer he replied, 'No one has ever been able to establish a connection of partnership with her, she has rejected all the offerings ever given to her.'

Normally, Storm was quite the strong and proud type, but for him to be speaking respectfully of another being for seriously surprising, even for me. It was probably the most astounding thing I'd ever seen since bonding with him.

Although he is only a teenager.

'So are you.' he replies smugly to my thought.

Sometimes I really am ready to curse the mental link I share with Storm.

'You only have one heart, be careful who you decide to give it to.' I warn defensively.

'You too, Rick.'

He says before settling down for the night.

Before I retired to sleep I saw the Angel escapee join Melody in their chosen tree of rest.

I caught a flash of blonde hair streaked with varying shades of blonde and hazel, and the sparkle of sea blue eyes faded to green and then finally glinted silver in the ghostly moonlit night.

The angel sang a song of great sadness that held a captivating beauty all its own.

It's voice gave me the impression that the 'it' was a 'she.'

As they settled in for the night I signal Storm and the pack as we leave to return back to the camp.

Storm and I take to the sky as silently as shadows, leaving behind a faint trail of rustling leaves and stirred branches.

We land back at camp with the moon at its zenith,

and, surprisingly, Rose is still awake, and as I walk by she whispers something so quiet, even in the near stillness of night my ears have to strain themselves to catch her words.

I had no clue what she was talking about but her voice was filled with memories of sadness, pain, loss and regret.

She rises gracefully, leaving me to ponder her statement in eerie silence as the night grows older and the starlight starts to dim.

I can only guess at what she meant by "Let her stay." I was really too tired to focus though.

I finally fall asleep against a tree, the moon mirrored in a rippling creek, her eye wavering continuously in the running water.

CHAPTER 3: MYRELLE - TWO TIGER CUBS

When I came back from the lily pond Melody scolded me soundly, saying, 'You can't sing every night Myrelle, it's a danger to the both of us.'

She was so worried about me that I agreed only to sing while in flight for the next two days.

I immediately regretted this deal, when Melody kept telling me to be quiet.

To pass the time, since we had to stay near the human world until the full moon passed, I asked Melody, 'Why did you decide to bond with me?'

Melody considered the question before replying.

'You are a royal and that impressed me. You were always full of surprises, so when they let the captured predator flyers out and opened all the cage doors I immediately heard you whimpering. You didn't cry or scream like most all the others and I decided to help you. You were and still are a pure angel. You haven't done anything for your own benefit; you were always thinking of others and of me over yourself.' Thinking momentarily, she decided to add, 'You did everything you could to make others happy. I thought it would be good if something was done for you for a change.'

Chuckling quietly, she also said, 'It surprised them quite a bit when I was the one to help you. After all my parents were forced to bond with someone of power from birth. I am glad I chose you; you are my friend and that is a much better deal than I could have ever hoped for in a bonded angel companion.'

Considering this thought quietly, we descended into a suspenseful silence, during which leaves of every shape and hue darted in our way.

At this realization, it struck me to take a look around.

Sure enough nearly all the leaves had fallen off the trees,

and those that still clung to life on the trees innermost branches trembled slightly as a howling wind set in. 'Melody..?' I asked carefully, my tone ringing with a silent warning.

'I know.' she replied, showing me the best place to land and seek shelter that was nearest to us.

Making a swift descent, I crash through the thickest part of tree foliage before unfurling my wings to catch the updraft and slow my fall to earth.

A commotion in the thicket to my left makes the grounded leaves swirl around in repetitive circles before settling around Melody's hooves, softening the sound her hooves make on the ground.

Before I can ask her why she landed specifically here,

playful growls come our way and two tiger cubs roll out of an evergreen bush next to Melody,

clawing playfully at each other while one gripped the other's ear happily in her jaws.

11

What caught me by surprise was that one of them was a very pale orange, while the other, was a perfect snowy white.

Stranger still was the loving expression that could be seen clearly on Melody's face and the protectiveness she displayed towards both these young cubs.

Realization sunk in.

'You saved them, didn't you.'

It wasn't a question and Melody's slightly guilty expression confirmed my suspicions.

'You know the dangers of going off on your own; what if you were seen by humans or, even worse, an angel hunter!'

For once I was the lecturer and Melody was the disobedient horse.

'Be quiet.' Melody said sternly.

I wasn't listening anymore.

I didn't even notice when she pricked up her ears. I felt betrayed and exposed, how could she jeopardise the only hope we had of staying free from the claws of tyranny that continuously threatened the both of us! The instant I spotted the nearest clearing I took off and went to the burnt area. Quiet sobs escaped my constricted throat as I remembered everything that had happened over the last week and a bit.

Looking after Melody and myself was hard enough but having to deal with the memories of all those screams of pain, those terrorized expressions I'd seen for over three years at the institution and then losing Lily was really pushing me to my limits.

Melody, she must be worried about me.

How selfish can I be!

Taking a sharp turn in the air, I speed back to where I'd last seen Melody, halfway there I spot her in the distance flying towards me. She waits at a bare tree and I quickly apologize for my rude exit and obnoxious behaviour. She accepts my apology and tells me she heard voices and foot steps close to where we had landed.

My mind instantly flashes back to the two cubs, so trusting and loyal how could I have forgotten them too!

The sun is sinking towards the horizon and I can't help but remember my dream, as we fly over the familiar trees, the sun hits the horizon and I watch, fascinated, as the entire world changes.

Leaves turn fiery red and orange, twirling towards the ground as if performing their own unique dance before leaving the world behind to live without their brilliant splendour.

Trees glow with all different shades of orange and the ground is enveloped in a blanket of pink turning purple as the sun slips below the earth's boundary. With the last rays that disperse from this side of the world we find ourselves in twilight surrounded by a clear sky sprinkled with sparkling stars.

Seeing a number of stars blurred by smoke, I discern a faint glow that symbolizes fire.

Informing Melody of my intent and discovery I head towards the glow to investigate, completely forgetting about my earlier concerns regarding my vision.

As I near the fire, a shape flies towards me and before I know it a blanket and net are covering my wings and I am falling through the air.

I wake up to hearing Melody's anxious whine.

Trying to smile reassuringly at Melody I feel myself wince instead.

I blink repetitively, trying to get used to the sudden brightness; the sun seems to filter though a window or glass panel.

I sit bolt upright and look around me frantically.

Realization soon sinks in as I realise that I am in a portable angel prison.

I can distinguish the presence of minuscule air holes.

Hearing a rustle is the bushes my head whips around to see a pair of knowing, chocolate brown eyes that look upon me sadly...

CHAPTER 4: RICK - ANGEL ESCAPEE

Storm lands before me gasping for air; he looks exhausted and in desperate need of sleep.

'She's... awake.' he pants breathlessly.

Work mode immediately kicks in.

Storm had been the one to capture her using his sensitive sense of smell and hooves to work the Net-Launcher.

I still hadn't seen her in person.

As I beheld her for the first time my heart missed a beat and I barely heard Storm mutter, 'Star-tied idiot.'

She is amazingly beautiful with blonde hair that shines in the filtering sunlight and darkens with each layer you see.

It ripples just over the lowest part of her shoulder blades.

Her lips are a pale pink like a newly budding rose and her skin looks tanned in the midday sun.

Her eyelashes are long and thick; they're a pale hazel colour.

Her eyes took my breath away; they were sea blue with swirls of jade and flecks of silver and gold that flashed brightly in the sun.

Storm surprised me by stepping out of the shadows and into the girl's view.

"Storm! What are you doing here? Where's your bonded angel friend?" she asked aloud, both happily and suspiciously.

He responded into her mind and she stiffened in fear. Her resolve held however and she answered, "No, I won't tell you my name."

Storm said something else and this time she responded, "I'm fifteen."

Still Storm looked helplessly at her and returned to join me.

'I was asking her that for an hour before I came to get you.' he said.

'Why were you so out of breath if she had been awake for such a long time?' I asked through gritted teeth.

'Because she wanted a companion since her bonded angel animal couldn't be seen in the vicinity.' he growled at me.

'So that means...'

Before I could finish that thought, I hear a cry of "Melody!"

and a great wind brought me back to the present world.

Sure enough Melody landed right next to the Angel and tried to make the gathered berries she had go through the glass angel prison.

However, the enchantments placed on the cage stopped her.

An expression of awe wandered over Storm's features as Melody managed to enlarge one of the air holes and drop a few of the smaller berries into the cage.

Storm's expression was quickly replaced by something akin to a smirk.

'You look like a fish out of water Rick, might want to introduce yourself and me to Melody.'

Regaining my composure, I stride out onto the field only to come face to face with a very angry Melody.

She spoke directly into my mind saying, 'Let. Her. Go.'

Annoyed but not surprised, I introduced myself and Storm 'Hello Melody. My name is Rick from Angel Haven, son of Martin and Maria, the royal tailors of Angel Haven. This is my bonded Pegasus, Storm, born to Lucinda and Ralph of the fire plains.'

This caught both Melody and the Angel off guard.

Specking directly to Melody this time I stated, 'I would like to talk to your angel friend alone for a while. Is that alright with you?'

Melody snorted and took off in the direction of Honeydew plain.

Storm followed her at a good distance leaving me to talk to the captured angel. I approached her cautiously and her eyes never stopped looking at me.

"Will you please tell me your name?" I ask her, trying for a polite approach. Unfortunately for me, she isn't thrown by it.

"No." was her firm reply.

Her voice was sweet as honey and sounded like a creek, gently rippling over its bed, though at that moment it carried an edge of exasperation and determination.

"I came here to visit the shining pool when the blue moon reaches it's culmination and receive my gift."

Why she was telling me this I didn't know, but she was definitely special if she needed to visit the Ocean to receive her power.

"Why did you leave?" I asked, curious despite myself.

"To escape the tortures of seeing other angels suffer, and I couldn't leave, I had to escape!"

She turned towards me and I saw tears glinting in the corners of her eyes.

"The Institution has walls higher than the tallest trees and layered with deadly poisons so that even if you reach them you will die. The roof is crisscross barbed wire and there are so many different traps hidden in the air and ground it's nearly impossible to escape."

Anger and pity welled up inside me and I muttered, "At least we were smart enough not to send Rose there."

The Angel perked up at hearing the name Rose.

"From what they told me Rose seems to be a wonderful girl." she said.

"Who told you about my sister!" I exclaim, alarmed.

"The tigers of course, Sarah, Sebi and Crisanta."

"If you're a common Angel, than why do they want you back?" I asked, confused.

"If only I knew all the answers to that." she sighed.

A sudden movement made us both tense up and that's when Sarah burst from the bush and started talking really quickly but of course neither of us could understand her.

Then I hear Rose screaming, "Rick, help!"

I was in action immediately, leaving the Angel alone in the Cage.

I flew towards the sound and found my superior holding Rose above the ground by her hair.

Tears streamed down her face and screams as well as sobs caught in her throat.

"Let her go, Sophia." I roar at her.

She ignores me, as we'd been taught and states her message.

"Here's the deal, you capture and bring us the pesky little Angel in half a years time and we'll let your family live, if not then you won't ever see your parents again. Once a full year has passed your sister will be coming to the institution with us.

Got it?" she sneered at me.

I can't formulate a verbal response I'm that shocked, but I manage a curt nod, my eyes, smouldering coals of hatred as I glare at Sophia.

Rose came back to camp with me and saw the Angel for the first time.

"Why did you cage her up!" she screamed at me. That surprised me, considering she'd been held by her hair not a few minutes ago…

"Its alright Rose, the tigers told me all about you and your brother, at least I'm not back at the institution yet." came the faint reply from the Angel.

I have something for you, but, could you please call Melody back for me?" she asked.

She sounded so weak, and then I remembered, she hadn't had anything to eat or drink for an entire day. The berries were the only thing still sustaining her! Cursing myself for my forgetfulness, I give her some water, which she drank gratefully. I may be her captor, but I wasn't someone who tortured and taunted his charges needlessly.

Melody is there within seconds after Rose calls her and soon the Angel is feeling much better.

"We have a gift for you Rose, if you'd like to have it." says Melody.

"Yes please." Rose replies and then from the pocket in her top the Angel removes a gift the size of a finger and whispers her strength and Melody's magic into the parcel.

"Open it when I wake up." she instructs before curling up and falling asleep.

I watch her serene face from the shadows, silent as can be.

She's a stranger, but considering that Rose seems to know her, somehow, I'd say we've got a shot. I mean, we've broken the rules a few times already, what's one more time going to change?

CHAPTER 5: MYRELLE - THE ANGEL-ANIMAL

Rose is very trusting, basically the exact opposite of Rick.

He has chocolate brown hair streaked with hazel. In comparison, Rose has strawberry blonde hair streaked with golden blonde and fiery orange much like a contained fire.

Rick has eyes that swirl with all shades of brown imaginable with a few flecks of jade visible when the sun hits them.

Rose's eyes are completely green in colour, verging on turquoise when the light strikes them, rare flecks of gold and hazel can be seen in her eyes.

Both of them have slightly tanned skin.

Rose has lips that are full, a rich pink in colour, and a voice that sounds like a playful breeze, always present, sometimes more noticeably than others.

Rick's voice shows authority and kindness simultaneously.

'His parents made my favourite dress.' I think, awed by their craftsmanship.

I awake to the sound of playful laughter.

Sunlight filters through the cage and I see my two captors and new acquaintances playing Fly-Frisbee. It looks like a lot of fun.

Smiling slightly, I sit up and the memory of last night hits me, hard.

I remembered the gift for Rose and my promise.

I hope she likes it.

Reassuring myself with the fact that she is a good friend to three rare tigers and is still a pure one, I sit up and begin my meditation on the past events.

Memories of fun, hurt, loyalty, pain, fear, kindness, love, happiness and other emotions well up inside me as I remember what happened to me not two days ago.

When I open my eyes I find myself face to face with Rose's smiling face.

"She's awake!" Rose squealed happily.

Laughing despite myself, I ask her to go and fetch her brother to which she eagerly complies.

I see Rick long before he lands in front of me.

"What do you want?" he asks me, slightly irritated.

"I want to be let out so that I can fulfil my promise to your little sister." I reply coolly.

"Forget it, Angel," he scoffs back at me.

"Fine, then let your sister suffer the loss of an angel-animal." I shoot back.

This clearly surprised him as he froze on the spot before sneering, "That's not possible, only one of pure nature has the power to grant connections to a bonded angel animal."

"Well then I guess you've never heard of me." I retorted angrily.

Before he could think of a comeback Melody and Storm appeared between us and Storm opened the hidden gate that imprisoned me.

Outside the cage an open-mouthed Rick and a joyous Melody greeted me. She immediately spreads her wings, preparing to take off into the thicket of the forest.

I shake my head slowly, indicating my decision to stay with them.

Melody looks at Rick with an angry flare of fire blazing in her eyes. A quick and soothing explanation stops her from losing her temper and transforming into the thing that had saved both of us when we escaped the institution.

Meanwhile, Storm was facing a stern lecture from Rick.

Breaking the silence, he yelled at Storm, "But you let her escape!"

This accusation made Storm wince slightly, at both it's tone and volume.

"Actually, I'm still very present." I confirmed.

Startled at my sudden intrusion, he turns around to face me, shocked.

"Now please let me focus so that Rose may have her gift." Disbelieving that I had remained where I was, he complied and Rose gave me the parcel which I had given to her the previous night.

Flying into the sun, I levitate the parcel on beams of sunlight as my mother had taught me, circling the parcel slowly and leaving it to hover in the sunlight. Then, using the water from a nearby lake, I began the process of collecting air moisture to wrap the parcel in mist.

Once I finished that the parcel stayed where it was before exploding outwards with black, yellow, green, gold and white coloured streaks revealing a leopard cub angel animal.

'I knew it'd have something to do with cats.' I thought as Rose gasped, admiring her new friend before meeting its green eyes flecked with gold.

The cub purred loudly and began the bonding process, growing its new wings, which were cream coloured, flecked with honey tones, hazel and a bit of gold; they also had a green tinge underneath them.

"I love her." Rose sighed happily.

"What're you going to call her?" I asked curiously.

Thinking for a moment, she talked to her angel-animal for the first time, and her eyes lit up as she told us that she wanted to name her angel animal Jade.

"That's a wonderful name!" I said enthusiastically. Now all we needed were some tears of happiness from Rose.

It really wasn't very hard to collect a couple of tears seeing as how she was already crying happily while admiring the newest addition to her family plus Jade was all hers!

After dripping the tears onto Jade's wings and forehead, she was able to fly, if a bit wobbly, above us.

Happy beyond comparison, Rose's every movement and expression was filled with joy for the rest of the day. I really hadn't expected my freedom to last, thinking Rick would just put me in the cage again and this whole event would be forgotten.

Considering the amount of trouble he was in for keeping me here over these last two days, I would have been willing to bet he would march me right out of the Humans Forest and bring me back to the Institution.

Rick was still just gaping at me though, as if this entire day had just all come back and slapped him in the face.

He whispered quietly, saying, "How?" before full on glaring at me and asking, "How the hell did you do that?"

I was so shocked at his outburst that it took me a moment to find my voice.

"I told you I was a pure one, but looks like you need to work on your ability to trust."

I was not about to tell him anything else after insulting me with such a stupid question.

"Do Melody and the Jade still have their trackers installed?" he quizzed me.

"No, I took them both out myself before springing out of that prison." I retorted, annoyed.

Did he really think I was that stupid?

He was treating me as an equal when I was princess of his home.

He doesn't know that though, I reminded myself quietly.

"When does the blue moon rise?" he asked me.

The change in his tone was enough to make me tell the truth this time. "It'll rise in six days on the seventh night." I recalled after seeing the moon half waxing the night before.

"Alright then, we'd better head for the ocean. It's a good three days flight from here, if we don't have any carry-ons."

I cut in before he could continue confusing me, "The ocean..?"

I felt stupid since I was supposed to know about this stuff but I was really curious about this.

"You know… the shining pool is also known as the ocean in the human world."

Still confused, I pressed on, "So why am I going there..?"

His expression darkened for a moment before clearing again, saying, "Because you need to be free from the institution just like Rose needs to be protected from harm."

"So you're saying Rose has to go home to her parents and you're going to take me to the ocean?" I quizzed.

Taking a deep breath, he replied, "Yes."

19

CHAPTER 6: RICK - A CHANGE OF NAME

'What the hell am I doing?' I think angrily as I make my way over to Rose to inform her of the change in plans.

'When I get home my parents are going to kill me!'

I'd been very pessimistic ever since agreeing to accompany the Angel to the ocean, or as she knew it, the shining pool.

'She is not worth risking my life for some silly power!'

From my findings I knew the angel was special and different from normal or other angels.

The only problem was that no one I encountered or contacted would tell me her name, most of them claiming not to even know the angel herself. Seeing my sister ahead, I changed my expression to a friendly one before settling into a crouch next to her.

Her gaze was fixed on something in the sky and at first I didn't even notice the leopard cub's presence until she flew through the foliage above me, settled into a crouch in front of Rose and hissed at me. Casting a look at Rose, she told the cub that I was a friend and not to be harmed.

"You have to go home." I stated bluntly.

She shook her head saying, "I won't let you take her away."

Her retaliation surprised me somewhat, since she normally did what I told her to.

"Why not?" I questioned.

"Because Misty told me to stay close to you and her." she replied.

"And this Misty is..?" I asked, voice rising slightly.

"She said that she was a friend and she definitely looked like an angel." was her only reply.

She got up and started walking towards the Angel's cage, pausing only long enough to tell me, "I think we should start trusting them." before continuing towards the angel. Of course I followed her; it's always been a habit of mine to make sure Rose is safe, no matter how strong she made herself appear to me. Sure enough she was kneeling outside the cage talking to the Angel in a hushed voice.

"...know who Misty is?"

Rose was finishing her question when I landed in the thicket to her right.

"Yeah, I'm actually surprised that she talked to you, normally she only communicates with me through my future seeing dreams..." the angel replied in an equally hushed voice.

Rose read the angel's expression of patience and then told her, "She spoke with Jade, and Jade told me most of the things that had passed between her and Misty."

"I thought as much," the angel confirmed with a nod, "but Misty has never led me astray so I think you should follow her advice...

By the way, don't bother yourself with the information Jade is withholding from you, she's just trying to protect you."

'She's very well educated for an ordinary angel.' I thought to myself.

Still, she had a very good point. Why wouldn't you trust someone who had never lied to you?

I was still confused as to why I was being excluded from the ongoing conversation but I couldn't dwell on that fact when I still had to convince Rose to go home, and the longer she stayed with the angel, the more likely it seemed she would come with them on the journey to the ocean or follow them once she was dropped off at their parents' house.

Taking off to make sure I looked like I'd just come from a perimeter check flight, I landed near the angel in the cage and said, "We all leave in the morning. We still have some things that need to be well hidden or brought back to our parents' place."

"I suggest digging a hole near a large tree and burying the belongings under that tree. The life source will made the materials harder to detect." the angel said, amazing both Rose and me with her knowledge of the 'hide and find' techniques.

"The institution doesn't let its pupils become stupid. In fact, we're better educated there than in any normal angel school." she said, then added, "at least that happens in our first year..." in a whisper.

Casting a glance toward her, I see such pain and loss in her eyes that I have to turn away before her sadness gets the better of me.

"She's been through more than either of us gives her credit for." Rose said to Storm, Jade and me, and for the first time in a long while, I believe her, and don't question her thoughts.

Before we left the angel she said, "Wait."

Rose and I both stopped mid stride and turned back towards her.

"I won't tell you my name for various reasons, I like you both too much to risk that..." she began.

"So?" I asked challengingly.

"So, you can call me by another name.

You can call me...

Myra."

CHAPTER 7: MYRELLE - FLY-BY MALL

Being woken up at five in the morning is not nearly as fun as it sounds.

For one thing it's freezing cold, you can barely see where you're going, and wearing a thin pair of jeans and a short sleeved top doesn't help you feel any warmer.

Although Rose had offered me her only jacket, I couldn't accept it because, first off, it wouldn't fit me, and second,

I couldn't bear the thought of Rose being cold while I was stealing her heat.

Rick had hidden their belongings under an oak tree that was near a pond, which was a breeding haven for white water lilies that filled the air with a wonderful scent.

Finding Rick was even harder than finding a shadow in the darkness, so, basically impossible.

A wispy cloud had just floated in front of the moon, momentarily stealing my sense of sight.

I would've walked right into him if the owl's sharp hoot hadn't made him flinch.

Just as I came up next to him the moon came into view, breaking through the cloud cover that had imprisoned it for the last few hours.

The stars were still gleaming palely as Rick asked, "Aren't you meant to be back at camp?"

"Aren't you meant to be looking out for Rose?" I counter.

That won me a slight smile from him before Storm and Melody came into view, the moon at their backs.

Funny, how Storm totally blended into the night but stood out in the moon's path of light while the opposite holds true for Melody. "What about your pack?" I asked, worried.

"I sent them home, they won't disobey me." he replied, surely.

"…How old are you?" I decided to risk that question.

"Sixteen…" and after a moment's hesitation he added, "Rose is thirteen."

Just then Melody landed next to me, speaking to all of us through our mental links, 'The faster we leave the more time we have before a tracker will figure out what's going on and follow us.'

"You're right, we should leave now. The darkness should hide our figures well enough and if we fly higher than normal we'll appear to be birds to the humans in daylight hours." Rick says aloud,

Before we left we told Rose the plan and took off towards the northern ocean since it was the closest and largest ocean.

Plus, I'd always been told that the shining pool was in the north.

I carried Jade for Rose since she couldn't fly as high as we needed to yet and was too heavy for Rose to carry while flying.

An hour later we were passing over a large town when Rose yelled, "There's a shopping mall down there!"

"What's your point!?" I yelled back.

"We could buy some more suitable clothing for you and me!" she replied.

She was already dropping lower towards a park opposite the mall, so Rick followed her after me, making sure no-one was awake yet or in the area of the park.

Jade wriggled out of my grasp as we neared the park, tripping over a stone when she landed. After her Melody and Storm landed on the gravel path as if it was the easiest thing in the world, annoying Jade to no end.

After them Rick landed to make sure Rose didn't hurt herself and then, finally, I landed next to both of them.

Rick gave me his trench coat to better hide my wings;

He argued that it was because his wings were darker than mine, but when I took the trench coat and my freezing hand brushed his warm one I saw him try to hide a knowing smile. He'd noticed I was cold and was looking out for me like he would Rose, and that thought surprised me.

Even though our wings are invisible to normal humans, anyone who interacts with magical beings will be able to see them. I don't' think I've heard of a single human who's been raised in ignorance of our existence either.

"You do know we don't have any money, right?" he asked Rose.

"I know, but Misty told me to go to the park and check under the bench on the left side."

Sure enough there was a purse with $200 in it.

"Why don't you ever tell me what's going on around here?" Rick asked, somewhat bewildered and annoyed.

"I'll start now if you'd like." Rose answered happily, already knowing she'd won this battle. She headed towards the street that had the mall on its other side, leaving us no choice but to follow her.

"She sure has taken a liking towards Rose." I mused,

"Who?" Rick asked

"Misty of course." I answered somewhat surprised that he hadn't caught on.

We followed Rose across the street and just as we reached the sidewalk on the other side of the street the sun came up over the horizon, casting everything into an autumn orange glow. "I think I'll wait for you two out here." Rick said, shocking both of us. He shot me a look stating he was testing how trustworthy I was and if I could protect Rose in a shop filled with humans. Talking to Rose I said, "Well, that means we get to spend fifty dollars each."

"What? Why not $100?" Rose asked, confused.

"Well, I don't like stealing and we need money to buy food and water." I explained, hoping she'd comply with my request.

"Alright then," Rose sighed, walking through the doors into an empty mall. 'Its only six am, no one is awake, and yet the mall's doors are open and the power's on.' I thought to myself.

Still, the emptiness of the place left me feeling queasy...

Finding a shop with teenage sized clothing, Rose was done buying her outfit in 10 minutes flat, paying $35 for the entire outfit, including a pair of cute brown boots, and, after leaving she was looking at accessories in every store we passed. I was starting to think there was nothing here that I would like when we passed a store called Sweets and Spice. It was very well organized and had amazing clothes in store and on sale.

The place was three dimensional, everything seemed realistic, even the things that weren't.

The store's wallpaper was pale blue with autumn leaves of every hot colour blowing through the illusionary breeze. Flashes of red, orange, yellow and pink caught my eye before disappearing to a different position on the wall.

When Rose and I entered she ran straight to the accessory display as she always did, leaving me to roam around the store.

When I reached the very back of the store, a young energetic woman greeted me and asked me if I needed any help.

"Do you have anything that looks good and also keeps you warm?" I asked.

"Sure, would you like something more suited to your figure?"
she asked, eying my thin clothing judgmentally.

"Yes please." I replied, after considering the offer momentarily.

I don't think that you're a dressy person but you love the colour blue, correct?"

"Yes, that's right" I answered, startled that she'd discerned so much out of my appearance.

"Well then, just wait a second and I'll get you something nice."
she said, smiling slightly as she disappeared into a nearby storeroom. With her gone, I went to check on Rose and found her admiring a necklace with a leopard's face and eyes made of jade hanging off a delicate gold chain.

"Do you like that?" I asked, startling her.

"It reminds me of Jade." she replied happily.

"How much is it?" I asked out of curiosity.

"Twenty dollars, I'm five short." she sighed sadly.

"Well, once I buy my outfit I'll see if I have any change left, okay?" I told her softly.

"Alright." she said, acting slightly more elated.

Not long after I finished talking with Rose the sales assistant reappeared with a box marked 'Blue and Beautiful.'

"I think you'll like what's inside." she said enthusiastically.

"Rose!" I called and soon after Rose came up next to me, looking at the box in my arms with curiosity.

"What's that?" she asked.

"An outfit I'm going to try on, will you judge if it looks good?" I asked her.

"Of course I will." Rose replied happily, looking energetic again with her new task.

Once I'm safely in the change rooms I open the box and gasp.

A single outfit is inside neatly folded up and piled atop each other in the order a normal person would put clothing on. The top was amazing, plain peach as the main colour resting on the sides of my shoulders with the neckline and bottom part of the top having a continuous swirling and dotted pattern of white printed onto it.

The jeans were breathtaking, a pure white with the lower part flaring around my ankles.

The jacket was the best part, a dark, yet bright blue dotted with three golden buttons, looking almost blazer-like.

The outfit completed had its own flare, showing off my thin frame and detailing every curve in my body.

Right at the bottom of the box was a pair of flat maroon boots that fit me perfectly with two golden buckles hidden by the length of the jeans, the shoes gave me a height advantage of two cm thanks to their heels.

There was a scarf in one of the boots; it was a bright yellow outlining some stars in brown thread. It kept my neck warm and felt smooth against my skin. Finally I came to the jewellery, which was a short golden beaded necklace,

and matching tight bracelet, the earrings were golden hoops, completing the outfit.

When I came out of the change room both Rose and the sales assistant sat there gaping at me for a full minute.

"I thought I looked rather nice?" I said questioningly to Rose.

"You look amazing Myra!" Rose said wonderingly.

"Thanks Rosey." I said sweetly.

"So how much is it?" I asked the sales lady.

"Since it's the only outfit ever made and suits you so perfectly I'll take $40 for everything."

"Thank you!" I said admiringly.

Rose was tugging at my sleeve so I looked at her and saw her puppy-dog eyes before remembering the necklace she had really wanted.

"Oh, could I also have the leopard face necklace with the jade eyes?" I asked.

"Sure, that'll be $60."

"Here you go." I said handing over the exact change and giving Rose the necklace before leaving the store and the institution's clothes behind.

Rose had bought plain black tights and a white top with a
shining design on it showing a pair of brown feline eyes and a
turquoise skirt, plus her leopard necklace.

"By the way..?" the sales lady asks, "are you two going to a dress-up party, because those are pretty noticeable." She points at our wings, and something told me she knew.

With a start, I remembered Rick's coat and rushed back into the store to grab it. When I walked out I checked out the woman's aura.

The aura was playful, polite and positive.

I sigh in relief before hurrying to catch up to Rose.

"Human's have a really weird currency, huh?" Rose says suddenly, mulling over her thoughts. "I mean, who asks for half the price of an entire outfit for a single piece of jewellery? It's just weird." I know full well she's talking to herself, and I can't help but smile as she continues to ponder the mysteries of the intriguing and yet dangerous human world she seems to know so little about.

We're about to leave the mall when Melody contacts me and states rather grimly, 'We're in a bit of trouble out here...' Setting off quite a few alarm bells in my head.

CHAPTER 8: RICK - HUMAN TROUBLE

Having Jade around turned out to be more helpful than I'd first thought. She was fast and agile, never running out of energy, much like Rose, attacking anything within her range except for Storm, Melody and me.

She was a blur of fur, fangs and claws and her size made it hard to catch her.

Melody and Storm were just as deadly, knocking people unconscious with their hooves and Melody also used her magic to make some of them fall asleep or turn on each other.

The whole thing had been a trap, made to look like a sleeping town, while humans lay in wait for the ripe moment to strike, when my guard was let down. They thought I was the lookout.

'At least Rose is safe.' I think grimly, punching another guy in the nose, making him stagger and his nose bleed.

The girls had been contacted by Melody before the worst of the fighting had begun.

Myra wasn't stupid, but she didn't know how to fight, as far as I knew.

Melody interrupted my train of thought then, saying,

'Myra is actually a very good fighter, she was top of the class in field training at the institution. Her trainer always recommended her as a Tracker, but, the request never got through.'

'Well she wouldn't stand much hope against these humans; she doesn't have the experience yet.' I told her, voicing my thoughts rather than using the mental link she'd established with me..

'Exactly.' she stated in return.

Throwing her a quizzical look, she explained. 'You said yet and that's true, but she will learn, from whom, I don't know yet, but she will, she always does.' Her thoughts quieten as she withdraws the mental link.

Just then I see a bush to my right moves slightly, and then a gust of wind throws the humans closest to it in every direction.

The diameter of the hit was too small to be made by Myra so that meant Rose had just taken off.

'What just happened?' I thought.

Before I could ask Melody what had just occurred,

Myra burst through the doors of the mall drawing attention to herself. She looked amazing in her new outfit, the blue immediately caught my attention and the jeans looked great on her ... Honestly, everything else she was wearing did too.

Her distraction gave the angel animals and me a chance to surprise the humans, and we took the chance as soon as it was presented to us, clawing, kicking and punching every human near us...

It didn't last.

One of my powers was very useful in this instance since I could shackle objects, living or not, using only my mind.

Before I know what's happening Melody and Myra took off, later followed by Storm and Jade, so I followed them.

"What's the plan from here?" I asked Myra.

"I turn up the heat." she said before turning towards the humans and yelling down at them, "Would you rather be hot or cold?"

"We'll have you come down here so that we can capture you and take you to the glass exhibit zoo, where you belong!"

One of the men yelled back at her, smirking under his beard. "Alright, I'll choose for you." she yelled back. "So, would you rather they freeze or boil?" she asked me.

"Boil sounds easier." I told her.

"Good, 'cause my freeze is far from good."

So she faced the humans once more and flew in a circle, encompassing all the humans present while keeping the sun at the centre before pointing at the sun and then at the human cluster, and the air started to heat up, showing heat waves and making the place look more like a desert in summer than a town in autumn.

"So you can manipulate heat." I stated.

"So you can restrain things with your mind." she replied.

Every time I think I've got an advantage over her she always evens the score out again.

Smiling slightly, we take our leave from the mall, leaving the humans to recover from their short-spent time in the oven.

I noticed, she let go of her power the instant she was satisfied with the result.

She didn't waste magical energy needlessly, nor prolong suffering in any form.

'She's obviously Pure too.' I think to myself, slowly starting to believe Rose and my new companions.

CHAPTER 9: MYRELLE - POWERS AND PROBLEMS

When we got to the park we asked Jade to locate Rose and within a few minutes she came out of a cluster of trees having been hiding in the uppermost branches the entire time.

"I'm so glad you're both okay." she said happily.

"I still don't know why the humans didn't see me take off though?" she mused.

"I wouldn't mind knowing that either." Rick stated, glancing at me.

"Okay, but if I tell you my powers, I want to know yours too." I told them. They both nod their agreement and wait for me to speak.

"So, my normal talents revolve around sunlight, heat and water. In fact, I control sunlight, heat and water," I said.

"So what about you?" I asked Rick.

"Well, you already know I can restrain items with my mind. I can also levitate objects and I haven't received my third gift yet," Rick told both Rose and me.

Rick and I looked at Rose expectantly.

"You guys have seen me communicate with animals,

but just last year I received a power that allows me to locate anything by only thinking about the item I want to find." Rose explained.

Continuing, I explain, "I'm different though, I'm given eight separate powers, but I can only gain the other five by visiting the ocean every year when the blue moon shines." Myra continued.

"No wonder the Institution wants you back so badly." Rick mused quietly.

"That's not the only reason they want me back, there are some more..."

I state decided to tell them what I'd learnt.

"I figured out two of the biggest secrets the institution has and they think I'm the key to unlocking at least one of them."

"Good thing you're with us then." Rose said, smiling.

"We'd better leave, before the other humans wake up."

Rick said, leading Rose away from the Park.

"Good idea." Rose and I agreed simultaneously.

We both laughed as we flew further north.

Endless fields of browning hills, desolate and devoid of life, the wind howling and moaning as if in pain. These were the first things I saw and thought when I beheld the Lone Plains for the first time.

"Do we really have to fly over here again?" Rose asked, wrinkling her nose in disgust.

"Again?" I asked Rick.

His only answer was a helpless shrug and a weary look at Rose.

"Yeah, we always go this way when we go camping, it smells terrible and the scenery doesn't change for ages." Rose complained, casting a pleading look at her brother.

"We used to go through the forest, but for a few years now, we've been avoiding them." Rose added helpfully.

Understanding flooded through me as Rose continued to argue pointlessly with Rick.

Angel hunters are posted throughout the Forest Path, they pick off lone angels and write them off as commoners!

Angel hunters are specially trained Angels that learn to hunt down and capture other Angels for a specific purpose or price.

Lily had told me she was a duchess's daughter but was listed as common because she'd been caught on one of the Angel World's Forest Paths.

There must be a lot of angel hunters there if they capture angels along the entire path... or, there's something on the path that needs to be hidden. Casting Rick an apologetic look, I intervene in their argument, "The sooner we leave the sooner the scenery changes." I say, smiling at Rose who rolled her eyes, clearly annoyed.

"Alright." she huffs before taking off towards the northern horizon.

Rick takes off without a second glance my way;

he's always on edge and doesn't really share his feelings. Which is the exact opposite for Rose, who loves to talk about everything and express her recent emotions as obnoxiously as possible, but she compensates for it with her good cheer and continuous optimism.

'Stop.' Melody tells everyone and we look around subconsciously, anticipating an ambush or sudden attack.

'We need to rest.' she states.

"No, we don't, we need to get out of the open as soon as possible." Rick snaps at us.

"Melody's right Rick, look at them, we need a break."

I say looking around worriedly.

Rose is kneeling in the dirt behind us gasping for air,

and next to her Jade pants loudly filling the silence held between Rick and me.

Both Storm and Melody lay in the dirt, tremors racking their bodies as the breeze turns to a strong wind.

"Come on, there's a cluster of trees a few kilometres from here, it'll shield us from this wind, at least." Rick yells over the now roaring wind.

So I scoop up Jade and we fly up vertically,

trying to escape the rushing wind, and once we break the cloud cover the wind dies away, and the sun warms us soothingly.

Slowly chasing away our weariness as if it were only a bad dream brushed aside carelessly, giving us relief, for the moment, from our troubles.

After a couple of minutes spent above the clouds we dive back into the fray of the storm. Raindrops sting my skin like acid and spread their freezing poison through my body.

We keep our wings pressed close to our bodies until the last possible moment before snapping them open and catching the created updraft before crashing through the trees and into a place of surreal beauty.

"This isn't the cluster of trees you meant, is it?" I asked in a whisper, afraid that even the slightest disturbance could shatter this image of purest tranquillity as if it were no more than a dreamt up fantasy.

"No." he answered, equally taken aback.

The trees were lush green, bearing fruits of every size, shape and colour despite the odd season for their growth. The grass was untrimmed and long, waving to and fro as the breeze flitted amongst it. It was like a never ending season of summer.

Water-splattered flowers cascaded shadows and sparkles over
a path trampled with boot prints, heavily indented into the earth!
'We're on the forest path!' I think, alarmed.
Something was amiss. The forest path, looked,
felt, and smelled wonderful, but the sound was terrifying.
There was none, a stony silence enveloped the forest.
Not a bird sung, nor a cricket chirped.
The leaves didn't rustle when the wind rolled through the trees and the breeze held no song.

The tromping of boots caught my attention and murmurs of conversation ran over us.

"We need to hide." I said quietly.

Rick looked confused at first but then his ear twitched slightly before he grasped an awestruck Rose by the hand and towed her after him.

"We should hide in the thickest trees." Rose whispered frantically, seeing our rush to leave.

"No," I cut in, "they'll expect that. We need somewhere protected, somewhere dark and low where it'd be hard to distinguish our features." I explained quickly.

The tramping was growing in multitude and volume.

"Where are we going to find something like that?"
Rose asks, exasperated.

"Right below us." Rick said.

I finish the sentence for him, speaking with a smile,

"Underground."

CHAPTER 10: RICK - HIDERS AND SEEKERS

"We should split up, then regroup once the angel hunters are gone." Myra said.

"We could meet above the cloud cover. If they're not fully trained it should be easy to lose them in the storm." I suggested.

"Done." Myra said. She was nervous, and scared beyond my comprehension, but Rose had suggested that she'd endured more than we knew and gave her credit for it.

"You two should stay together." Myra continued, looking first at Rose and then me.

"They're probably already following our footprints. I'll see you two in a while, good luck!" she whispered to us, and before we even had time to form similar words on our own tongues,

she was gone, moving with the grace and speed of a frolicking gazelle through the forest.

"Good luck to you too," I whispered into the empty space where she'd been standing a moment before.

She'd taken Jade with her, and for that I was grateful.

"Myra has Jade." I comforted Rose, who was looking around her, a confused expression on her face.

"At least she'll be safe with her." she sighed regretfully.

"We need to get out of the open." I said, attempting to distract her.

"What about up there?" Rose suggested.

Sure enough there was a small cave not 200 meters flight from where we stood.

"Well spotted, we'll have to hike there though." I informed her,

to which she replied with an annoyed, but hushed, groan.

~

Agility was always one of my strongest points,

and endurance ran in the family. It was just irritating having the same scenery running for miles.

'I need a vantage point.' I thought. For all I knew I 'd been running in circles. There was no way to tell if I'd been here before, because everything always looked the same!

Catching a glimpse of something grey, I climb the closest tree and catch sight of barren fields.

It was a graveyard of tree stumps wrapped in a blanket of smoke. In the distance a large fire burned, casting the entire place into a shadowy haze. The fires glow faintly outlining only the largest of objects.

~

We'd just reached the base of the mounted cave; the thickly growing bushes obscured the cave's entrance twenty meters above us.

"I'm not climbing up there." Rose states in a flat tone.

"Well we can't fly up there." I say in a mirrored tone.

"Why not?" she asks, irritated.

"Because there's a trip wire in the air halfway up." I say matter-of-factly.

"How do you know that?" Rose asked quietly, clearly fearful of capture.

"Because I'm standing right where the light hits the wire." I answer automatically.

"What's that then?" she says, pointing at something in the air.

When I stand where she is I see multiple other wires strung throughout the trees above us.

"Ok, we are definitely not flying up there." I confirm, seeing Rose start to blanch even more.

"What about below here?" she asks,

Sure enough, the stone near her foot was movable and underneath it there was a bowl shaped hollow, large enough to hold 3 fully grown angels.

"Hold on," I said, picking up a nearby pebble and dropping it into the centre of the bowl which slides apart revealing a tunnel going in the direction of the mountain.

"Hey, Rose, would you rather run or hide?" I asked, gaining an amused smile from her.

"Hide." came her practiced answer as she jumped in the hollow without so much as a backward glance.

~

Jade really knew her way around; she guided me through the bush as if she'd lived here her entire life.

'How do you get this information?' I asked, bewildered.

'I can flick through Rose's memory. She used to play hide and seek along this path when she was younger, we're just lucky we're going in the same direction.' Jade says, speaking through the mental link I'd established.

I'd been running for a good hour now, and I was really thirsty.

Hearing a bubbling brook, I head further to my left only to be stopped short by a yelp from Jade.

'Don't go that way, it's not a brook, it's a trap. Rose always avoided going left because all the animals told her it was dangerous.'

As weird as it sounded, it made perfect sense.

'Wait, I can't hear a single bird chirping and you're telling me there were animals here?' I asked puzzled.

'Yeah, squirrels deer, birds, butterflies and heaps of other insects too; they all left when their homes where destroyed though.' Jade added.

She really loved conversation as much as Rose.

'You mean, all the tree stumps I saw in the haze used to be animal homes?' I ask, horrified.

'Yep, they couldn't keep living in these trees because the leaves became poisonous to their skin. The other two are still above the tree line monitoring the Angel hunters for you by the way.' she continued cheerfully.

'Wait, you mean Melody and Storm are still looking for us?'

'That's what I said.' Jade replied.

'Melody!' I called out, searching for her.

'Myrelle! Are you okay? Where are you!?' came the eager reply.

'I'm fine, and so is Jade. I don't have a clue where we are but I think Jade might... where are you?' I answered.

'Back at the lone plains, above the cloud cover. Storm's with me too.' Melody answered happily.

'Storm!' I yelled into his mind, ripping open the link I'd once established with him like a newly received letter.

'Ow! What is it?' he asked, in a slight bit of pain.

'How do we get out of here?' I asked,
quieter this time.

'Find the silenced wood thrush, enter his nest, cross the border,
and fly free, is the riddle told to me.' Storm answered.

'Ask Rose, she's already up to crossing the boarder.' Melody added helpfully.

'Thanks you two.' I said before turning to Jade.

'Think you can contact Rose through rock?' I asked uncertainly.

'I can try.' she replied.

'Rose...Rose! Can you hear me?'

'Jade! Where are you, what's wrong?'

'Rose, I can't hear you, but if you can hear me,
get Rick to contact Storm. We need to solve the wood thrush riddle!'
And then she was gone.

~

Her presence vanishes as quickly as it came.

"Rick!" Rose said, alarmed.

"What?" I ask apprehensively.

"Jade contacted me, she said Myra has to solve the wood thrush riddle, and you need to contact Storm...now!" she continued.

So I did and as soon as he felt my mind against his he explained the riddle to me and I listened intently the whole time.

'So, you want Rose to contact Jade again and tell her where to go?' I clarified after the discussion.

'Yes, but Myra has to achieve freedom for everyone.' Storm explained quickly.

'Why can't Rose do it?' I asked, slightly offended.

'Because she doesn't have the experience needed. You know that more that anyone else; just wait for her.' Storm whispered before withdrawing our mental link.

"Rose, do you mind contacting Jade and telling her to aim high, look low and tread in the grey?"

I ask her.

Her response is obvious enough…

CHAPTER 11: MYRELLE - THE WOOD THRUSH RIDDLE

Aim high, look low and tread in the grey…

'What do you think that means?' I asked Jade for the hundredth time.

'Aim high, would mean either something really tall, or something in the air… Look low would mean that once we get there we need to find something on the ground, but the last line confuses me…' Jade explained again.

'Maybe it means shadows.' I suggest.

'I don't think so, shadows are black, not grey.' Jade stated.

'Lets look up first then.' I say.

'Good idea.' Jade compliments.

'What about that?' I ask, seeing a mountain with a cave looming behind us, intimidating even the largest angel animals.

'It's a good place to start.'

Jade answers, with a mental, indifferent shrug.

After walking for a good half hour we come to the mountain's eastern side.

Dusk is beginning to set in and the world is being drained of colour ever so slowly, leaving behind the stains of the sun's red, orange and yellow rays.

A large rock provides me with a seat on which to rest awhile. The stone suddenly starts to shift and when I get up and look at it again I can see that where I was sitting was in the curve of a bird's wing.

"Jade! I found the Silenced Wood Thrush!"

She immediately appears beside me as I push the bird aside to reveal his nest.

'Ok, so now what?' Jade asks, confused.

Enter his nest.

'We climb in, I guess.'

As soon as we were in the nest, the ground beneath us gave way to a tunnel across the border.

'We'd better start walking.' I sighed.

We hadn't walked more than a kilometre when we hear the sound of a poorly concealed sneeze.

'Can you contact Rose, to see where she is?' I asked in the confines of our minds.

'No problem.' came the cheerful reply.

'Rose, where are you?' Jade asked.

'Jade! I'm in the tunnel under the wood thrush with Rick, where are you?' she asked tentatively.

'Same place, we just heard someone sneeze.' Jade answered.

'Really? That was me! Stay where you are. I'll come your way.' she said, bubbling with happiness.

'You're further than us, come back towards the wood thrush and we'll see you soon!' Jade replied, mirroring Rose's happiness.

'Rose was the one who sneezed, she's coming our way.'

Jade relayed the message to me.

'Great, all we have to do now is wait.' I replied joyously.

Fifteen minutes and many hugs later we continued our journey to gaining our right to freedom together.

Rick seemed even more withdrawn than normal,

but other than that, everyone was happy.

Jade never stopped talking, telling tales of her birth that those who are older cannot recall.

How she had combined her needs with Rose's wants and become the leopard cub she was now.

Plus, because she's been in contact with Rose while she was still in her spirit state she had developed some of Rose's characteristics as well.

'Like your optimism and love for conversation?' I asked.

'Yea, but not just that. I have her boundless energy and agility too. Rose is more a sprinter so I'm really good at releasing short bursts of energy.' Jade continued proudly.

A flicker of light caught my attention up ahead and just as I was about to ask what it was the sticky lava pool came into view.

This is an inactive volcano!

"No wonder it was getting so hot." Rick said.

That made Rose roll her eyes. "No big deal, we'll just fly across." Rose said, already half spreading her wings.

"No." I say sharply, stopping Jade from unfurling hers.

"It's a bursting pool." I tried to explain.

"What's that?" Rose asked, somewhat puzzled as to why we couldn't just fly over.

"When the sticky lava feels a heat source other than its own it releases a burst of lava towards that heat trying to quench its competition." I recite.

"So... How do we get across?" Rick asks, startling us with his sudden interference.

"By confusing it enough that it gives up trying to shoot us down." I say, smiling.

"We fly in a random pattern above it as fast as we can and while it's distracted we get Rose and Jade across." I said, glancing at Rick to see if the plan worked for him.

"Sure, let's get flying." he agreed.

"We'll call you when it's safe enough." I call over my shoulder to Rose and Jade.

"I'll keep them safe." I whisper to Rick.

"Don't make promises you can't keep, Myra." Rick said.

"Ok, I'll go first and once you see me do it find your rhythm and follow suit, okay?" I asked.

"Lead the way." he replied.

Remembering my father's lectures, I took off and started slow, making sure the lava noticed me before finding my own rhythm again.

I started my complex dance with the simple twirls and leaps at first as lava rained down around me. I moved both with and independently of the lava.

As the lava's frustration grew, my evasion became faster and the dance increased in difficulty. It was at this point that I called out, "Come on Rick!"

And he came, his movement was slightly off and slower than mine but still good enough to evade the bursts from the lava below us.

He made it to the other side and instead of continuing he stopped and watched as I leapt, twirled, flipped and circled and still he remained where he was.

A rumble of desperation emanated from the lava and the central burst was released in a last desperate attempt to quench our flames over his.

I easily avoided the blow, dancing to the side and skirting the entire cavern in a spinning frenzy.

Finally a whimpering growl signifies defeat and I called Rose and Jade over. They complied, if rather hesitantly…

"Come on! We need to be fast if the lava is to remain confused." I yelled at them, but they weren't fast enough.

A pleased gurgle emanated from the lava as it assailed us with many more bursts. Rose and Jade cowered next to each other.

I flew towards them as fast as I could, pushing them out of the way as another burst assailed them. This time I flew across the alcove like an arrow shot from a taunt bow string, taking the two girls with me.

The sticky lava wasn't stupid though.

It aimed ahead and shot a burst directly at Rose, attempting to weigh us down.

Swerving at the last second, the burst struck my left wing tip instead of Rose.

Using some more of my strength, I threw both Rose and Jade at the entrance on the other side, struggling to get there myself with one of my wing tips clamped to my body.

Seeing both of them make the distance, I focus on keeping myself in the air.

A shadow falls over me and I see Rick flying down towards me using the technique he'd learned while watching me.

'He learns by sight.' I realized, that was why he'd landed on the other side and watched me. Now he swooped below me, caught me in his arms and flew me up to where Rose and Jade waited for both of us.

"Are you both okay?" I asked, concerned if I'd hurt either when throwing them to the other side of the cavern.

"We're fine, thanks." Rose replied for Jade and herself.

"Are you okay?" Jade asked hesitantly.

"I'll be fine once we get to Melody, but there won't be anymore serious flying for me until then." I added sadly.

Seeing remorseful expressions cross Rose and Jade's faces,

I quickly add, "It wasn't your fault, I'm glad you guys can still fly."

Rick then asks, "So... what now?"

I quirk an eye brow at him before answering that;

"Isn't it obvious..?

We keep fighting for our freedom."

CHAPTER 12: RICK - FIGHT FOR FREEDOM

Myra continued leading us through countless other tasks knowing the solution to every problem presented to us. Though she couldn't fly she was still incredibly quick and nimble using agility, memory and wit as her primary sources to solving the riddles presented to us. Now we were faced with a simple but non-accomplishable task, fly over the pillar lake.

The problem wasn't that she didn't know what to do; it was that she couldn't fly with only one wing.

The pillar lake was an agility course where you used your wings to stay above the water pillars and fly to the other side, continuing the fight for freedom.

Myra had been communicating with Melody for the last ten minutes, arguing about the best course of action to take.

Finally Myra opened her eyes, scanning the course with such focus I was starting to wonder if she was okay.

"Rick, Melody thinks she can lend me her wings for a short while. I need to complete the course as quickly as possible,

get there first to warn the girls," she said quickly.

"Ok, will you be alright?"

"When I finish this task I will be." she whispered quietly.

The course was easy, two loops in the middle, a few avoiding spins here and there and you were done.

When Myra did it, it looked like a swan gliding across a lake except it must have been five times faster than any swan could ever swim. It was amazing to watch. She was done in seconds and her wing resumed its original form as soon as she landed next to Rose and Jade.

Melody had accomplished an amazing feat; she was an incredibly strong and skilled magic user especially for her age.

Wandering further down the tunnel, we see moonlight filtering through an opening...

We'd made it.

"We're not done yet." Rose and Myra spoke at the exact same time.

'Must be a pure one thing.' I thought,

"There's one more test to pass." Rose continues.

"We need to find a clearing filled with grey sky and leave

through there." Myra finished for her as they smiled at each other.

"Right, where are we going to find that?" I asked sarcastically.

"Above the next alcove, if the riddle is anything to go by."

Myra considered.

"We'll need to look out for angel hunters too, you never know where the next trap is going to be." Jade added hastily.

"Knowing them, if they actually do see us they'll just run off to report to their superiors and organize a trap where they'll have the advantage. They probably think we've been caught somewhere already anyway so I wouldn't worry too much…"

Myra reassures her before saying, "Well then, we'd better get going."

A pinprick of light, swirling, darting and dancing, was visible above us.

This alcove was far from small but there were no words that could have properly described its height. The towering mass of stone made us appear no more than dust specks in a cleaned house, small, yet incredibly important in some areas.

A tangled spider-webbed maze of wires gleamed menacingly in the moon's waning light, making it impossible to tell where they were positioned.

An idea, fleeting and desperate, darts around my head verging on impossible but definitely worth attempting.

I explain it to the girls. "If one of us can find where the wires connect to the stone we can find a safe flight path through the maze of wires, and you"

I said, gesturing towards Myra.

"Should be able to rock climb past the wires at least; I can fly you further up if your strength fails once you surpass the wires' position." I explain further.

"Alright, but who's going to look for the placement of the wires?" Myra asks questioningly.

An awkward silence filled the chamber as we each considered our advantages over the wires.

'I think I should go.' Jade thinks, startling us out of our thoughts.

'I'm agile, fast and the smallest of our group.' she explained, laying out her various reasons.

"Rick, you should tell Jade some tactics for evading traps should she trigger any of them by accident." Myra suggested thoughtfully.

"Wait! What if she does get caught? She shouldn't risk herself for us. We're the ones who dragged her here, not the other way round!" Rose interrupts hastily.

She was extremely protective of Jade, and for good reason too.

"There is no better option available!" I growl at her.

"Myra can't fly, I'm too big to fit through the gaps in the wires, and you are a young, pure angel.

Were you to fly in Jade's stead you would be caught immediately. Jade is not a full angel and she is pure, and that gives her an advantage of luck that we would otherwise lack!"

I yelled at her, trying to get my point across and calm myself.

"Rosey, do you really think you could do this better than Jade? She has many more advantages over us and you could learn from watching her. You don't need to experience something personally to know how to avoid the dangers that it poses." Myra explained gently.

She was very kind to her, with large, soft eyes, a demeanour that displayed an endless patience, and a moral integrity that was pure and positively optimistic. "Fine, but Rick has to give her the knowledge of at least three different types of avoidance strategies," Rose sniffed quietly.

Smiling despite myself, I sit down next to Jade and explain several strategies of avoiding capture should she trigger a trap accidentally.

"The most commonly used tactic is 'sense and fly.' You need to be aware of all your surroundings. If you even brush a wire it could be triggered, so, when you feel the wire's pressure you need to fly vertically and fast, at least in this instance," I explained slowly.

"The other two have a lot to do with endurance and agility you need to confuse the tracker. The tracker either searches for movement or heat so you need an abundance of movement lasting for as long as possible to confuse it enough so that it shoots the trap randomly instead of accurately, very similar to the sticky lava." I continued engagingly.

I was so engrossed in my lecture that at first I didn't notice Myra's' absence until she called, "Guys... these aren't trip wires, this is a spiders web... Belonging to a real spider!"

she called down, starting to panic.

"These threads are as viscid as fresh glue!" she cautioned.

"Don't touch the threads and you'll be fine; this is an agility and communication test." she continued before her eyes lit up like a lamp had just been flicked on in her head, and before any of us could stop her she jumped off the ledge she was on.

Heading towards the nearest thread and turning her body mid-air, the sticky lava burst, caught onto the delicate thread, peeling back as if it was no more that a snake shedding its skin.

"Come-on!" she yelled down at us after to see if a trap would be triggered.

Unbeknownst to us, one had triggered itself, and the spider waited patiently, for its prey to be caught in her woven trap...

CHAPTER 13: MYRELLE - GAMBLING GAMES

Silken threads were strung everywhere. None of us had gotten caught yet, but a suspicion clung to me like a leech clinging to its only source of warmth.

The moment my wing had been free I'd kept flying up,

but no mater how fast or far we though we flew we made no progress in our struggle and as another set of chills ran up my spine, a fearful idea entered my mind.

We're being watched.

The spider is hiding here and we're too blind to see its camouflaged hide!

Irritation seared my body as I scanned the walls for the slightest movement that would give her position away and yet again that fatal clue evaded my gaze.

Yet as we neared the wall to rest a slight discolouring in the rock that had eluded me before suddenly became visible. "Stop!" I cried, alarmed.

They did, confused expressions crossing their faces as they turned to me for an explanation of my sudden outburst.

"The spider is right there." I said in a quiet, wavering voice, pointing out the slight discolouration in the wall behind them.

This made their eyes widen as Rose said, "She's right, I've been feeling her presence ever since we cleared the first set of threads. She's hungry, but, there's a stronger emotion in her that I can't quite distinguish, it's as if she wants to hurt us and wants us to reciprocate her movements."

"That means she's either anticipating something important or wants to play, most probably both," I explained.

"We don't have time to play." Rick snarled like a wounded animal refusing to admit his mistake.

"Yes we do." I snap at him.

"If we can gain her favour she might not eat us and if we're really lucky she'll let us go."

That matter cleared, Rose slowly flew towards the discoloured area and gently tapped the spider near the head.

"Would you like to play a game?" Rose asked, illustrating each word with calm and care.

"Sure, what do you want to play?" she asked happily, her voice resonating with pleasure that she'd been found and was being included in our discussion.

It was a voice that rustled like silk that fell to the floor in slow motion, and dry autumn leaves that flipped and twirled in the early winter wind's song.

"What do you want to play?" Rose asked her sweetly.

"Hmmm, something to do with chasing," she declared, shifting her position slightly and revealing her true size in doing so.

Her size was about half as big as a fully grown dragon, which meant she was very big.

Jade would have been easily squished by one of her feet.

She was at least ten times larger than me when you counted her legs.

"How can you understand me?" she asked, confused.

"It's one of my angel gifts." Rose replied honestly.

This made the spider hiss venomously.

"I hate angels." her voice resonated in the cavern, making the very walls shake.

"They are destructive and mean; they silenced this place, killing the birds song with their homes."

Hearing a faint tap, I follow the sound to a small alcove nestled in the wall opposite the spider;

a single nest with two eggs in it was hidden there.

Meanwhile the spider continued her story, "Six months ago a pair of birds came here wanting to return the eggs they'd been sworn to protect, but what they found, was their worst fear. The trees and birds dead and dying the father only had time to utter a single name before passing into the void. "Silky." he'd coughed, so the birds bought the eggs here, and I've cared for them ever since."

"No, you haven't. They're dying," I said, filling the cavern with my voice.

"That's not possible, the birds said they would hatch themselves!" the spider screamed in my mind. "They cannot hatch without heat and sunlight!" I shouted at her angrily, sensing that she blamed herself, I add in a softer voice, "I can help them if you let me."

"How?" she asked tearily.

"By using my powers of heat and sunlight, but in return we want you to let us leave and I need to be outside for my magic to work anyway." I answered cautiously.

"No! You cannot leave this place." she yelled, irritated.

"Then let the young birds you so love die in their shells!" I yell at her.

Seconds rolled into minutes as Silky and I held the silence she'd created.

Finally after a defeated whimper of, "Help them…please." She let me pick up the nest and she carried both the eggs and me to the upper entrance.

The sun was just rising past the horizon when I flew into the dawn's rays and levitated the nest on the first rays of day

then, drawing the heat out of myself. I gave the eggs my body heat and the sun's full morning energy.

At first the eggs shook, then they vibrated, and finally, they cracked.

44

As the shells disintegrated two young birds hatched forth;

one was pure white speckled with spots of hazy pink, orange and yellow beneath her wings and stomach; the other was a vibrant purple with flecks of bright pink, orange and pure black beneath his wings and stomach.

He had a pure white diamond on his forehead while she had a black tinged purple diamond on her forehead.

"Dawn and Dusk." I whispered to them and with a sharp snap their eyes opened revealing two sets of sky blue eyes.

"She is Dawn," I said, gesturing to the white bird. "And he is Dusk." I said, gesturing to the other.

Before Silky could respond a song of such joy rushed over the forest as we turned and saw Dawn testing her voice on the sleeping forest.

Her voice projected life, love, joy and awareness in every living creature that heard her song chasing away the last of the night's shadows and letting a ripple of such intensity pass through the forest, conjuring life in every form for the earth to the sky that it looked as if heat waves radiated from the mountain's point.

In contrast, her brother's voice sung of whispering breezes passing through sleeping cities, artifice images of mourning, longing, sadness and isolation preparing the world for the coming night.

His very essence was the exact opposite of his sister's and yet they existed in perfect harmony.

When they sang together every being present shivered at the recognition of the balancing forces befalling them.

Hovering before me they spoke, their voices echoing with happiness and hope.

Dusk had a voice of such sorrow the sky began to weep, letting its tears seep into the earth.

Dawn's voice vibrated with summer's songs from the creek's gentle ripple to the breeze's soothing whisper and they said,

"Thank you, healer," before touching their diamond foreheads to mine and reciting, "You saved our lives, and thus we are in your debt, so here is our gift to you."

A golden spark flickered into existence, floating around me.

It started to glow, growing brighter and warmer with every circle it drew around my body.

Finally, it drew its final circle around my neck and a golden locket settled coolly against my throat.

"Our gift to you … healer." they whispered before flying off into the sunrise, a trail of new growth following them below.

"Healer?" I whispered, confused.

CHAPTER 14: RICK - HIDDEN GIFT

Two days had elapsed while we where stuck in that mountain and obvious joy was displayed at our safe return. 'Myra! You're alright!' Melody squealed at her in the confines of her mind, accidentally including all of us in the conversation.

Laughing at her childish enthusiasm, Myra answered,

"Of course I am, those bursts were a breeze for me."

Storm showed more restraint than Melody, keeping his emotions hidden behind a thin impassive mask that I knew had taken years of mastery.

Surprising him and me, Myra give him a tight hug,

smiling the whole while. The whole thing was just too good to be true.

"Hi! Are you okay?" she asked quietly.

He wriggled out of my constricting grasp, eyeing her curiously before turning to the exuberant Rose. She gave him a tight squeeze, launching into a detailed account of the horrors of the underground world.

"That locket holds much power," Melody observed, sniffing it curiously. "Will you open it?" she asked.

"We'll see…" Myra answered carefully.

"Yeah, will you open it for us?" Jade piped up happily.

Unnoticed to all of them, I was looking straight at Myra and I finally figured out what had changed.

"What?! " she snapped, irritated.

I could see she would've added more if I hadn't been looking at her with that weird expression.

It was as if all my pretences just melted away leaving my face open and honest though a trace of seriousness was still visible, or so Rose described it later.

"Your hair?" I whispered, awed.

Flying down to a nearby pond, she reflected the water with some sunlight gasping as the ripples ceased.

Her hair was still the same golden blonde but the waves had been replaced with luscious curls that cascaded over her back. "Since we're already on the ground I think I'll open the locket Dawn and Dusk gave me," she stated out of the blue, a barely audible shaking to her voice.

~

With clumsy fingers I click the latch open and feel a rushed heat race through my body. My fingers are seared from the locket's scorching metal but the weird thing was, it didn't hurt

at all.

When the bright light finally faded I touched a wound I saw on Melody and when my fingers came in touch with it, it healed.

'So that's what they meant by Healer.' I think, finally understanding what the two birds had meant when they'd said that.

When I opened my eyes again Dawn and Dusk hovered right beside me.

"You've opened our gift, so we've come to show you how to use it." they stated simultaneously.

"Thank you." I whispered, honoured.

"Your hands control direction, where you touch you heal, as you discovered with your hands."

They began each instruction simple and direct.

"Your thoughts have to be focused to direct the level of healing,

be it skin, muscle, ligament, or bone."

~

They continued, worrying her, since she though her focus wasn't that good.

Reading her expression, their voices become soft and reassuring.

"Don't worry healer, your focus will intensify the more you practice your new skill." they crooned.

So when she wanted to heal skin, muscle, ligaments or bone, she had to think of the place the injury was, how deep the wound went, and how severe the injury was.

The one thing that puzzled her she wouldn't say, but the discomfort was plain to read on her face.

She seemed to be fighting inside herself before deciding to give us the knowledge that troubled her so.

It was the fact that she had to discover her heart's song and sing it, whether in her head or out loud she was still unsure,

to heal a broken bone or alleviate emotional pain.

A heart's song was the very essence of who an Angel was,

so if ever she did discover it she would keep it to herself for as long as possible.

Later that day a storm brewed in the North, it was decided to cover as much distance as possible before the full force of the storm hit us.

Taking to the sky, our mood changed with the clouds above us.

At first we were thrilled to be in the air and together again then as the sky darkened, Rose started complaining and even Myra grew silent as the rain and wind set in, determined to separate us and keep us from our goal.

The rain stung like a thousand needles piercing our exposed skin and chilling us to the bone.

Before the rain got any harder Myra created a protective water-based sphere, keeping the rain off us and turning the storming weather into a pleasant, if cool, breeze.

Though the sun didn't shine, our spirits soared as we searched for a place to land.

We'd been flying for just over an hour and our enthusiasm had just now started to wane as we desperately scanned the ground for a suitable place to make camp.

Our strength had been sapped by the cold,
which has worsened since we encountered a stronger headwind.
Something's off…water droplets seep through our barrier,
forcing their way onto our clammy skin, sending freezing shivers running up my spine.

Instinctively I look towards Rose. She looks fine, if a little pale and cold.

A mental cry of 'Myra!' and a flickering shadow falling steeply towards the earth startles me, as my thought trail leads to her.

"Close your wings!" I call to everyone just as the water barrier dissolves, letting on the true strength of the storm and sending us spiralling towards the ground.

Storm takes my meaning instantly and with a yelp of surprise both Jade and Rose just managed to fold their wings before they were sent plummeting towards the ground.

'Myra…' I thought suddenly craning my neck over Rose's shoulder and seeing a single figure falling towards a cluster of trees with Melody flying right behind her, and in the blink of an eye Melody's forehead star glowed white hot.

In a blinding flash of pure white light time froze.
Rain drops hung suspended in the air all around us,
as if each was being held by an invisible thread.
In that moment of time freeze, Melody catches Myra on her back.

Beckoning to us, 'Don't just hover there; let's get down to that cluster of trees before the spell ends.' she insists before rolling her eyes impatiently.

I'd been so shocked at the change of environment around me that I hadn't even noticed we weren't affected by Melody's magic.

Angling towards the cluster of trees Myra had been falling towards only seconds before, Rose, Jade and I all flew and landed in a slight parting of the branches of the largest tree while Melody headed straight for the ground. Confused at first, I follow her down to the clearing where she carefully landed and bent her head as an invitation. Realization swept through me as I saw Myra laying flat across Melody's back.

Careful not to disturb Melody, I pick up Myra and lay her gently against a nearby tree.

An hour later Melody spoke, filling the silence in the confines of my mind.

'You like her, don't you?' she asked softly.

'What does it matter? She'll just go back home once she gets her new power…' I sighed, finally giving up my pretences. Yes I liked her, most everything about her intrigued me, but more often than not it felt like we were worlds apart. Not to mention the nagging fact that she wouldn't tell us her real name left me feeling all kinds of suspicious… and worried.

Upon the conclusion of my thoughts, a spark appeared above my head swirling around me and turning into a beautiful flower as it settled in my hands. My eyes wide, Melody says, 'Looks like your Natural gift finally found its place.' Accompanied with a whinnying chuckle.

'You knew!?' I asked, both infuriated and surprised.

'Of course.' was her mentally smug reply.

CHAPTER 15: MYRELLE - JADED THOUGHTS

My head spins as I try to sit up, groaning quietly.

I open my eyes to find myself on one of many white dunes that mark the beginning of the white desert, which, in turn,

will level off to the Ocean and the Beach.

'We have two days to fly over this.' I thought, worried.

My spirit rose seeing Melody, Rose, Jade and Storm glide towards me, the sun watching their backs as night turned to dawn.

Rose squealed happily when she saw me standing on top of the dune. Plunging toward me at a sickening angle, she wraps her arms around me.

I gasp at her body temperature and realize that each of them had taken turns in using their bodies to shade me from the merciless desert sun.

'I'm out of the ashes only to be burning like a fire.' I think grimly before realizing what I'd just thought.

It's still only one verse, though I couldn't help feeling proud of my heart's first verse.

I realized with a start that Rick was assessing me from afar. Thankfully the sun's heat mostly concealed my blush.

"We should get going." I encourage everyone only to be regarded with blank expressions.

"The blue moon rises in less than a half a week." I say,

nerves gnawing at my stomach.

Standing stiffly, Rick speaks, his voice washing over me in waves of patience, "We've been searching for the hidden path but we can't find it." he said, an edge of bitterness entering his tone.

"Well that's easily solved, we just have to wait for sunset."

I said patiently, hoping he caught my meaning.

He did.

"We can't survive much longer in this blistering heat." he answered through gritted teeth.

"Then you forget our gifts." I answer back tersely.

Summoning my power, I create a literal water globe surrounding my companions, keeping the heat out but letting the light in so they could see what surrounded them.

"Since we have the time why don't you entertain us?" I asked Rick smugly.

He raised his eyebrow questioningly and it was Melody who interpreted my meaning this time.

'You should teach us how to fight, or at least Myra and Rose.' she explained, her patiently rubbing thin.

Rick was a great teacher, instructing me in my pose and technique and noticing every flaw in my positioning.

"No." he says exasperated

"Fly into the sun but then attack your opponent, if you stay still too long you'll become visible to your opponent." he continues, frustrated.

So for the fifth time I jump into the air, keeping the sun to my back and this time I attack him.

When the dust clears I open my eyes and find myself face to face with Rick.

His eyes are blazing brightly, but when he noticed me looking at him the fire dimmed to a glowing ember.

Annoyed, I push myself off him and mutter, "I think Rose needs to improve her landing position." before turning on my heel and marching off to the edge of the water barrier where I recite the first verse of my heart's song, "I'm out of the ashes only to be burning like a fire." Without even noticing at first I added, "The wind seems to whisper, as twilight starts to shine." Confused, but hopeful, I utter the two verses under my breath and find the breeze stirring to the words.

Leaping up, I find Melody looking at me knowingly.

Then, something changes, her neck stiffens and her muscles start to tremble.

I'd seen this before and its meaning back then hadn't been good. Seeing fear in her eyes I start to seriously worry,

something wasn't right.

With a hiss that cut through the building silence, Jade's fur rippled and stood on end as her gaze fixes onto a point in the sun.

Slowly I make out ten flying forms and see the glint of steel and worse, gold.

"Those are Catchers!" I say, starting to tremble with fear.

Rick notices my still figure and immediately spots the fear in my eyes.

Looking past me, I turn and see Storm pawing the ground and tossing his head nervously as the figures get closer.

"Catchers!" he yells at all of us. First he places a scared Rose onto Storm's back and whistles shrilly.

At the sound of that whistle all the bonded angel-animals take to the sky expecting our immediate departure after them but all I can do is watch the figures slowly growing in size as they get closer to us

"Fly!!!" I call desperately to the angel-animals as they take off at full speed towards the tangled forest.

'Keep them safe.' I think, sending my thoughts through the wind to catch and speed their progress.

Glancing to my left I notice Rick was still on the ground next to me, his eyes burning with pure hatred.

Glancing my way, he seems taken aback at my presence. "Aren't you staying with Melody?" he asked sarcastically.

"No, I'm going to dishonour them." I say, jerking my head towards the oncoming catchers.

Caught by surprise he said, "You do know they're Catchers, right? The only person who can command and even dishonour them is a person with the status of a Duchess or higher."

I already knew that but I wasn't about to dishonour them by legally taking their honour.

"Yeah, so? I'll teach them to fear me again." I say, accidentally letting the, again, slip into the sentence, and before he can comprehend my meaning I take off towards the Catchers,

just as the sun hits the horizon and the first sign of day's end and night's arrival occurs.

A golden light bursts forth from the horizon illuminating the hidden path.

Rick called strongly with his mind, 'It's a trap Myra!'

But by then it's already too late as I feel the dart pierce my neck and the world around me turn dark…

CHAPTER 16: MYRELLE - TRAPPED

It's cold and damp, the cell seems familiar but my head still swims with memories of capture.

Standing up I realize with distaste that I am once again clothed in the institution's student uniform only this time I'm wearing the peasants clothing, the mini skirt and top.

As my head clears I realize that it's dim, dark and damp because I'm in a cave. Walking forward, I bump my head against an invisible barrier. Cussing, I feel the microscopic presence of air holes. Looks like I've been locked up in a portable angel cage again. Hearing a groan of pain, I turn around and see Rick lying against the cave wall.

"Rick." I whisper, before all out yelling, "Wake up! We have to get out of here, wake up!"

I try to touch his head and find another barrier blocking my path.

Despair grips my heart as I frantically bang on the barrier separating us, and then I see it.

Blood trickled from a wound in his head; multiple bruises cover his body. What's worse is that with something separating us I can't use my power to heal him.

I hear chatting voices and see the ten catchers enter the cave, somewhere to my right, allowing anger to fill every fibre in my body, I glare at them as they enter one at a time.

"Looks like the little one's awake." One smiled evilly.

"At least we won't have to worry about that one."

another said, flicking his wrist towards Rick.

The one who spoke saw the spark of fear enter my eyes.

"Yes, he was very protective of you." he muttered, turning, and I saw that all of them where covered in bruises similar to Rick's.

"Must be siblings." another grunts.

I later learned that the leader's name was Mike and his companions all had names starting with 'M' as well.

"What are you going to do with us?" I squeak, playing the part of the scared little sister while sending my approximate whereabouts to Melody using the wind and water to send my thoughts to her.

"You, are going to go to the institution school?" Mike said, gesturing to me.

"He's going to the Seeker Training Arena."

He continued gesturing to Rick.

Hope flooded me before I saw the looks the guys were giving each other.

"What Mike forgot to mention was the liberties we get to take on the girls we catch." One called Marcus added gleefully.

He was obviously the one who liked to take such liberties with his captives. With a start I realize my wings had been tied up, and so were Rick's. "And how do you expect to do that?" I asked, all presences withering like a mask slipping away, revealing some of the real me.

"See! I told you she had some fight, and that fight is awfully sexy." Marcus crowed, grinning towards me.

"To answer your question, we simply make you do it, or we put you to sleep."

So the chain was used.

I was told it mostly relied on hypnosis.

My mother had never told me how to avoid its effects so that was a slight problem.

Just as I thought this Rick stirred, slowly, he blinked and when he saw me alive he seemed to relax a bit.

"Yeah, we haven't done anything to her… yet." Marcus hissed, eyes flashing angrily.

Rick still wasn't quite awake and he soon fell asleep again.

Hopefully he'll wake up ready to fight, I thought, worried.

Seeing a glint of gold, I turn my attention back to Marcus, which was probably the worst thing I could have done.

The chain hung limply from his hand and when he saw me notice it he began swinging it gently to and fro while chanting,

"She will do as I ask, she will obey me, she will be helpless until I release her."

He repeated the words ceaselessly, the problem was that no matter how hard I tried I couldn't look away from that gold chain. It just held my attention, swinging back and forth,

back and forth.

After a minute he took a step back and I involuntarily took a step forward.

I was too focused on the chain to notice Marcus's evil grin. Barely noticing what I was doing, Marcus walked me right out of the cage and into the arms of his two companions. While one held up my head the other poured a dreadful tasting liquid into my mouth and the whole while the chant continued,

"She will do as I ask, she will obey me, she will be helpless until I release her."

I gagged on the drink but never took my eyes from the chain.

Suddenly, the chanting stopped and I heard a loud snap then Marcus's voice rolled over me saying, "I am your lord and master, you shall obey me and do as I ask."

He guided me to a wall where chains hung right next to Rick's cage.

"Chain yourself." Marcus ordered, and I did. A small part of me was still aware of what was happening around me and desperately tired to snap me out of the trance. My Royal blood was already fighting the drink and I became more and more aware of my surroundings, I felt like a freak'in doll, something living that did not seem quite alive. And it was horrible.

Marcus was already in front of me,

his hand tracing icy patterns across my skin.

When he reached my thigh I froze. He straightened and stared me straight in the eye. His eyes were a dark forest green flecked brown, like a murky swamp. Snapping back to reality, I kicked him, hard. Glad that I'd only chained my hands.

He swore loudly causing Rick to wake up. When he saw me his eyes hardened and he opened his cage, exclamations of astonishment and confusion rippled through the other eight M's.

Rick ran really quickly, but he wasn't fast enough. Quick as a whip Marcus had me by the throat holding me above the ground.

A pained whimper escaped my constricted throat causing Rick to pause long enough that some of the men regained their composure.

Kicking Marcus in the abdomen, I drop to the ground, gasping for air.

Springing up, I locate Rick, surrounded by six of the M's while the remaining three went for me.

I uttered a bark of mirthless laughter as the others tried to encircle me.

"You really think he's a bigger threat than me?" I asked them, savouring the confused expressions that light their features.

"Don't you recognize your own princess?" I whispered to them, taking my two little satchels from my pocket.

I emptied the glittering contents into my palm and twirled. My movements matched those of a gazelle: fast, free and graceful.

The whole while I let the magical sparkles dance around me, and then the cave was alight with a blinding white light that revealed a princess wearing a knee length strapless dress, which was the colour of an apricot, tinged with a dusky pink.

A golden tiara dotted with sapphires and diamonds gleams upon her head and a single sapphire diamond necklace is set around her neck.

Her hair runs down her back in curls of blonde with turquoise streaks.

She was Princess Myrelle Blue Sapphire known to her companions as… Myra. As the glowing light receded Myrelle found the 'M' group had fled the cave.

Only Rick remained…

CHAPTER 17: RICK - HIDDEN TRUTHS

Opening my eyes once the light had mostly receded, I find myself looking at Princess Sapphire.

And like a puzzle clicking into place all the clues fit together to reveal what had been happening all along.

'At least she didn't outright lie', I thought, gazing upon her.

She herself seemed to be in some sort of daze.

'But why couldn't she tell us she was Princess…?'

Before I could finish the thought Myrelle looked straight at me and I froze.

"Don't think it, don't say it, don't even mouth it." she whispered.

Casting her thoughts towards me, she repeats 'Myra' over and over again.

"Myra." I whisper and she relaxes, a trace of a smile lingering at the corner of her lips.

"So, how do we get outta here?" I ask, a hint of sarcasm in my tone.

A full grin transforms her face as she becomes the old Myra again. Then something miraculous happens, she starts to laugh.

I'd hear her giggle, chuckle and seen her smile and grin but never had she laughed like this.

Her whole face was transformed by that sound, her eyes glistened like freshly fallen snow.

And her voice sounded like a harp, soft and delicate rippling over me.

Of course I know she's laughing because we managed to scare off our foes.

"We trace the 'M's' path, obviously." she said.

Her eyes were still glowing happily.

A gentle breeze stirred her hair and she stiffened in response to what was said.

"Melody and the others just ran into the 'M's." she hissed, eyes flashing darkly.

I straightened at hearing this only to groan in pain as I applied pressure to my broken leg.

In response to my pained groan Myra snapped back to reality and her expression became fearful and sympathetic.

"Let me heal that for you." she said gently and without even asking she placed her cool hands on the exact spot where my leg had broken, and began to sing.

Her voice echoed through the caves as she wove the strands of music into the parts of the song she knew, singing of her very essence.

A tingling sensation started at the spot where the leg had cracked as she sang, "I'm out of the ashes only to be burning like a fire; the wind seems to whisper, as twilight starts to shine."

She'd whispered these very lines to herself while we were out on the sand dunes.

And now she added, "Heaven is calling, as our essence streams above."

All I could do was stare...and with a sharp snap the bone was healed, but it wasn't only the thing that she healed.

Because she'd sung a part of her heart's song any wound that had been inflicted upon me from the moment she'd met me vanished, as if they'd never existed in the first place. A little trick Dawn and Dusk hadn't mentioned while explaining the works of Myra's gift.

"We'd better get going now." Myra said. She seemed to glow in a light that emanated from her.

After a quick body heat search we found the tunnel the M's had used to escape from Myra.

Looking her up and down, I wondered at how I could have been fooled by her appearance.

She carried herself with such regality it was almost impossible to miss that she had the stature and grace of at least a duchess's daughter.

Her clothing had returned to its former state and so had mine. Our normal clothes once again clung to our backs. Noticing my gaze, she turned towards the tunnel leading out and walked away from me, and like a dog on a leash I followed her.

Gathering my courage and dignity, I asked, "So, why the name secrecy?"

Seeing her reaction, I bit back my next sarcastic statement. Her back was as straight as an arrow and her eyes seemed to cast a shadow of fear over her face.

Trying to get her back to normal, I add, "Don't worry Myra,

yours is the only name I know and I wouldn't call you anything else while we are amongst ourselves and friends."

A hint of a smile touched her lips, but it was but a shadow's shadow in comparison to her heartfelt laugh which had echoed through the cave only moments before.

As we neared the exit we heard a chorus of curses and a terrified scream that raised the hackles on the back of my neck.

'Rose!' I thought, filled with fear and a protective urge to help her but a nagging tug at the back of my mind stopped me.

Myra was looking at me with such intensity I froze and the nagging conscious grew until I could make out the thousands of individual thoughts buzzing around there, but they weren't mine... they were Myra's!

Somehow her healing had bound her mind to mine and vice versa.

Smiling despite the circumstances, she glared at me as I said, "You won't be needing wind messages with me around anymore."

Her glare only intensified as she struggled to keep some secret from me.

Confused, I withdrew so that only a tendril of thought and feeling remained between us.

She seemed to relax a bit when I left her to her own mind.

Another shriek broke the tense silence between us as we snapped back to ourselves.

"Apparently it's possible for the mouse to make the cat run away as well." Myra smirked; it was a common saying amongst our people and was all the more surprising because of it.

She flew off in the direction of the commotion,

but I'd sensed something else, a distinctive but subtle throb of a plant's conscience.

Following the plant's life song I enter a hidden chamber which I would never have been able to find were it not for the plant's directions, and that's when I see it—the plant was a blue lotus that I was very familiar with.

Instead of the sky-blue colour its petals were a vibrant but dark blue, like the night sky just after the sun had set.

And at the slightest motion it closed its petals.

When I reached out and touched it, it relaxed at the knowledge that it was safe and its petals opened with the sound of rustling silk.

My amazement couldn't be compared to anything at that moment.

The inner centre of the flower was a startling white amidst

the dark interior of the cave and the teal-coloured flecks were

also a sight to behold staining the white circle.

But the most amazing aspect of the entire flower wasn't its

petals or even its colour, no, the most amazing thing about this plant was its pollen which literally GLOWED with the pinkish haze that can only be seen during sun rise and sun set.

'Thank you for giving me life, Rick.' a soft voice quietly whispered into my mind, but no one else was in the cavern except the flower and me.

The flower sensed my hesitation to leave and let one of its petals blow into my hand.

I knew why the flower had seemed so familiar now, it was the flower I'd instinctually created when Melody had given me my natural gift.

Using the wind as a tool of transport it closed its petals again and another, more alarming thought entered my mind. 'Wind…Myra…ROSE!!!'

Fast as I could, I half ran half flew out of the cave,

right into the midst of hell…

Rose was flying circles around two of the M's, making them easy prey for Melody and Storm,

'There were ten of them before though…that means Myra's fighting the other eight with only Jade to assist her!' I think, panicked.

The other eight had managed to encircled Myra.

Marcus attacked, basically blinded by anger, a slight smile tugs at my lips…

'Girls will do that to you.' I think, making sure to block the thought from Myra.

Said Angel is a flurry of dodges and attacks, but, when she notices me her eyes widen a bit as she remembers something, widening the mental link I realize she's remembered the sun technique.

'She's crazy, there's way too many of them for that to work!' I think, awed and afraid for her.

Just as the sun breached the horizon she flew above the circle and said, "With the rising sun's power, I punish you for your crimes against your princess." And she began to glow until she was shining like the brightest star in the night sky before the light faded and she began to fall.

'Not again…'

I think, already diving after her.

CHAPTER 18: RICK - MISTY IN ALL FORMS

Swooping below her, I caught Myra in my arms, stemming my wing beats to lessen the impact on her and me.

Watching her in this unconscious state, I wonder if she could ever come to love a commoner like me.

'With my luck and her beauty she's probably got princes begging for her hand on their knees.' I think sarcastically and then another thought hits me.

Her mind was completely exposed in a state of unconsciousness. I could easily find out what I needed to from her.

And, not to mention, that secret she was so desperately hiding from me before.

Even after all we'd, I'd sacrificed for her, she still didn't trust me.

Lowering her down gently, I give in and sigh, defeated.

Rose looks at her and exclaims loudly as a wavering form appears before Myra.

Shifting my weight, I stand before the illusive image watching for a movement of attack, and then she speaks, 'You needn't fear me Rick, I bring urgent news for the princess.'

"Who are you, and what is so important you must disturb her whilst she recovers?" I ask, genuinely bewildered and annoyed.

'The blue moon rises tomorrow and you are a two-day flight from the ocean, she must get there. SOON.'

The illusion seems to shimmer before disappearing altogether. "What was that about?" Rose asked. She sounded about as bewildered as I felt.

The girl had been young, her wings only just reaching their flying point.

'Misty?' Myra's conscious suddenly seemed very alert and present.

"That was Misty? I didn't know she was so pretty; she looks a lot like…" she trailed off, gazing into the distance.

"She looks a lot like Rose." I finish for her.

And it was true, the resemblance was stunning,

both had the same heart shaped faces and bodily shape.

The most striking resemblance though, was their hair, both had fiery hair which was long and wavy, but while Rose's eyes were green, Misty's were sky blue, flecked with gold. Rose's eyes had flecks of hazel, Misty had green flecks. Rose had more angular and feminine eyes while Misty had large circular ones, similar to those of an owl.

Both had rich, full lips though Rose's had a paler pink in contrast to the peachy colour of Misty's.

"Why show herself to us now?" I wonder aloud. I could see the question in everyone's eyes.

"We have a bit of a situation…" Rose stammers, following her gaze. I see a swarm of insects lining the horizon only…

"Those aren't insects…they're seekers!"

Jumping up from the ground I realized that Misty had added a double meaning to her message.

We'll have to split up.

The reality of having to relay Rose into the care of Storm again hit home. Having my nerves on edge, I made a snap decision.

"Storm, take care of Rose and Jade I'll meet you at point A." Surprise flickered through Storms eyes.

'The Beach.'

"Melody, I'll carry Myra and we'll head for the Ocean, we need to get there very quickly."

'You want me to speed you up with magic?' she thought gleefully.

Nodding my consent, we left, two groups flying in opposing directions.

'Why don't I try a little trick on the two of you?' Melody queries.

I cast her a searching look.

'Won't you be accompanying us?' I ask through out mental link.

'Don't you know a magician never tries her latest trick on herself?' she responded teasingly.

'What… Wait!'

But her star was already glowing, the landscape was changing swiftly, blurring and forming indistinct characteristics of the passing environment and all the while I held onto Myra, making sure she was safe and warm.

The winds used in that spell were merciless and freezing. When I finally felt solid ground beneath me, I see that the spell worked, partially.

We were some miles south of the northern beach and the sky was clear, free of form and sound.

Looking down at Myra, I finally admit to myself that I really do love her and shrug off my jacket to keep her warm through the rest of the night while I lay down next to her and watch the stars and their constellations come to be and fall away as time continued to ebb and flow according to the whims of fate.

'Rick..? Rick. RICK!'

When I finally open my eyes I see a startlingly bright blue sky before turning to see Myra still asleep next to me.

'This is confusing.' I think.

'That's exactly what I think too.'

Giving a startled yelp, I realize Myra had been talking through our mental link the entire time.

'Why exactly did you have to contact me through our link? Couldn't you wake me up like a normal person?' I ask, first annoyed, then exasperated.

'Well I would've if I could've.' Myra retorted defensively.

'Sorry.' I cringed, 'Wait… what do you mean, if you could've?'

I ask quizzically.

'In simple truth, I can't wake myself up, for one reason or another.'

Great. That's just what I needed.

'Hello, Rick? Mental link remember…'

Shit.

'Right.'

I thought and moved away from her.

'Hey! Why'd it get so cold all of a sudden?'

When I touched her arm she remained motionless, unaffected by anything I did to her.

'Hello, are you gonna at least TRY to wake me?' Myra whined.

Breathing ragged, I try once more to get her physical attention by running my fingers over her face and straightening the stray, windblown strands of hair framing her face in a golden halo.

This time a muscle locked in her jaw and she began to shiver.

'Why are you touching me?'

Myra sounded a lot more secure than her thoughts led me to believe.

'To see if I could gain your attention…physically.'

Following my last remark her entire body tensed.

'Hey, relax would you? I'm not about to hurt you.'

She did.

A dangerous, but fun idea suddenly popped into my head.

'Mind waking me up?' I could have easily pictured her rolling her eyes at me while saying that.

She snapped, 'Now wake me up already.'

So I did, and I secretly savoured every moment of it.

From placing my hand under her chin, to tracing delicate neck and smooth shoulder, and finally kissing her to finish the job,

and it worked!

'That was your brilliant idea?!' she screamed into my mind.

"You can talk now you know." I say, dodging her mental assault.

This remark catches her totally off guard and she stops dead.

I can feel the conflicting emotions she's battling into submission until she finally looks up…and gasps.

"What?" I ask, discomforted by the intensity of her gaze.

'Have you forgotten your training so soon, Rick?' Misty says, smiling as I start, and look about to see her.

'I can see Myra's having a bit of emotional strife so I'll help 'break the ice' as they say.'

Looking back I notice Myra's gaze had intensified into an angry flare of boiling resentment.

'Look,' Misty said tiredly, 'Rick is in love with you and Myra is in love with you.' she said pointing to each of us in turn. 'Well, I'm needed elsewhere so ta-ta for now and remember to fly fast to get to the ocean.' she added with a wink before disappearing in a veil of fog.

As my gaze found Myra I could see her cheeks had flamed red hot and her eyes showed a fear that I'd only felt once before though I could sense an underlying curiosity too.

She really was a professional at hiding her emotions.

"Hey, it's okay. I'm sorry if I upset you…"

She looked at me then, like, really looked at me, as if she could see my very soul with that one piercing gaze. She took one unsure step forward then hesitated and seemed to make up her mind. She walked straight up to me and kissed me.

It was a glorious feeling finally getting what your heart had longed for, for so, so long.

Even if you yourself had only just realised your hearts desire not too long ago.

CHAPTER 19: MYRELLE - OPAL-LIKE SKIES

The greatest gift a girl could ever ask for is having the boy she loves love her back, but then there's always that nagging suspicion about the truth in his words.

During that kiss nothing existed except Rick and I.

Sensing his surprise, I stepped back.

He really was very tall.

I loved the mystical spark that appeared in his eyes when he got an idea or his training kicked in when there was trouble. I could sense his roiling emotions strongly as he battled each into submission.

I knew I was blushing so I looked down at my whitening hands clasped before me just as Rick's head jerked up.

When my hesitant gaze found his he tensed further, his eyes flicking towards me before looking back at the western horizon.

Intrigued by his focus and annoyed at his ignorance of me,

I look to the west myself. That's when it started, that terrible trembling.

I cannot believe a simple look at the sun could trigger it,

but it was happening, my conscious was fading, slipping away... but instead of emptiness there were pictures, flashes of colours and sensations all rolling together to form so many images.

A startlingly white palace against a pure blue sky, the scent of multiple foods for a celebration mixed with a sickening odour, only then did I see it...

Blood, dark and running freely over the marble tiles of the courtyard, and there she was.

"Misty!" I cried in anguish seeing my little friend slumped against the marble steps leading up to the palace.

"Go." she whispered meekly. "Leave me, you MUST save him."

And then I knew what this vision was of...I couldn't go back!

NO! This was impossible, and not to mention insane! Why in the world would I go back home? Why would I even think about returning to mum and dad at a time like this!? It doesn't make any sense!

"Rick..." she whispered before vanishing from my mind.

My eyes snap open to see a concerned look on Rick's face.

"You really ought to warn me before you do that." he stated, torn between concern, frustration and anger.

"Sorry." I smile weakly.

"So, will all that really happen?" he asked grimly, and in horror I realized what had just transpired while I was unconscious.

"You can see them too now." I groaned sympathetically.

"Yeah, and what I saw wasn't a good sign if the blood was anything to go by." he answered just as grimly as before.

"You didn't recognize her?" I asked him, surprised.

Now his expression was the one to grow confused.

"Was I supposed to?" he asked, deep in thought.

"That was Misty." I whimpered quietly, remembering my shock of seeing her there, not to mention the fact that she'd actually spoken verbally then and, worse still, the name she gave me afterwards.

Now he looked sympathetic and sad. "So she isn't a shadow after all." he said, trying to dry my dampened mood with his sarcasm, and it worked, partially.

"Yeah well, it sounded like you weren't having the best time." I teased quietly.

Big mistake. His entire body tensed and his eyes glazed over, as he seemed to recall something long forgotten.

"At least your people were entertained." he said dryly.

Now it was my turn to express my confusion.

"What do you mean by that?" Trying to explain the process to him I add, "When you fade into a vision you see through the eyes of the you in the future."

His mouth curved sardonically.

"Well I was in the arena of my birth city. Looks like I was being punished for some crime as of yet uncommitted."

Now my head cocked thoughtfully before my eyes widened in disbelief and shock as I realize what's going to happen to him.

Seeming to sense he'd hit a raw nerve, he changed the subject. "You know the moon should be at its zenith in a few hours,

we'd better get flying."

He gave me one of his rare melting smiles before declaring a non-spoken race on his behalf.

Yet even as I saw the tension ebb from his body I could sense his unease through our mental link as strongly as if it were my own, sending my thoughts into turmoil.

Suddenly Rick goes into such a steep dive I think we're being attacked and so I follow his movement instinctively.

He lands on the barren landscape with outstretched hands just as a baby blue jay falls in his outstretched palms, softening the impact of the collision.

With shaking hands, I trace the broken wing outline letting a spark of health and healing flicker over my fingers before murmuring my heart's song as softly as possible, healing the little blue jay's wing, and I sang, "I'm out of the ashes only to be burning like a fire, the wind seems to whisper, as twilight starts to shine, Heaven is calling, as essence streams above, trying to catch a falling star from the darkening night sky."

Smiling, I release the bird's wing just as its eyes flutter open, revealing opal-like eyes in almost every respect. Their shape was oval, like that of a jewelled opal, their colour was amazing, with a pitch black background and shining flecks of green, blue and purple.

'Hello little one, are you feeling better now?' I asked in her mind, receiving an acute glance my way from Rick before he gently lay the bird in my offering hands and took off to circle overhead.

Meanwhile the little bird's eyes had widened significantly before it finally found its voice again.

'Hi?' she answered shyly.

And as if waking from a dream, she began to flutter her wings, comforted by my voice and demeanor.

She squealed, overjoyed, 'My wing!...but how?'

Now she sounded scared.

'I did that little one, now what is your name? Mine's Myra.' The youngster seemed to struggle with herself. "My name?

'Well I think it's Opal but I must've hit my head somewhere because I can't remember anything else...' She sounded scared and ashamed of her memory. I understood her predicament perfectly.

"Hey, Myra, come see this." Rick called down, startling Opal out of her half dazed state and before either of us could do anything the little blue jay let out a shrill cry causing an explosion of light to my left right behind Rick, and who should appear but Dawn and Dusk.

Crying out in joy, I leap to my feet calling to the both of them,

"I should have known you two would be behind this kind of creation."

Their eyes locked onto me and their battle mode ebbs away, flowing out of them as easily as it had come to be in the first place.

"Myra."

They spoke with such sorrow and fondness they made me want to break down and tell them everything that had happened to me since I'd last seen them, but I knew that this matter had to be handled first.

"Opal, why do you call us to fight when these are our friends?"

Their presence and their proclamation left the young bird speechless and humiliated.

"Do not look so ashamed young one, tell us what cause you had to call us," Dawn spoke soothingly, emanating life and love, easing the little one's fear.

"He has wings."

she said as if it explained everything, and seeing her point hadn't come across, she tried to make me understand.

"The winged ones came and destroyed my home,

my siblings and parents are all dead,

their songs silenced forever."

A wave of sympathy threatened to engulf me as I listened to this little bird's tale of hardship.

"You must learn the difference between the good and the bad. His naming of her should have given you indication enough that they were both trustworthy."

Dusk intervened for his sister,

who had a distaste for negative protraction of speech.

So he dealt with it in her stead.

CHAPTER 20: RICK - THE BLUE MOONS GIFTS'

Flying at top speed with a baby blue jay in your hoody can sound like a great experience.

It just so happens to be totally deceiving.

Opal had decided to accompany us until she could repay Myra for her help.

She wasn't what I'd call the best passenger flyer,

she always wanted to look outside but then the wind made her too cold, she shared quite a few common factors with Rose in that sense.

Feeling a pang of grinding nerves I remember the last time I'd seen her that single flicker of doubt she tried so desperately to suppress.

'I just hope she's okay.' I think with chattering teeth.

Then we finally notice a subtle discolouration separating the sky from the sea. We had ten minutes before sunset.

'Are we there yet?' Opal asks for the millionth time.

She really is very similar to Rose. If only she were quieter when she spoke to us through our minds though…

Surprising how much time passes when you focus your thoughts inwardly.

'Come on Myra, we've got five minutes max before we reach it.' I urge her.

She tires very quickly when she wastes her power on protecting others.

I find a smile creeping over my lips as I remember all the times I've swooped below her to catch her when she literally fainted from her expelling energy, just to make it easier on us all.

'How can one being be so selfless?' I think, careful to avoid the inclusion of Myra's conscious.

'Pure ones.

I'll never understand them.'

My thoughts turn acidic as I remember that piercing feeling of losing a part of myself when I first thought of myself before those around me, abruptly ending my time as a pure one,

since we all start out as one.

'Rick..?'

Myra's conscious gently presses against mine, filled with an odd mixture of shyness, uncertainty and determination.

Her thought of concern is like a shaft of sunlight forcing its way through a cloud barrier, making me relax and drawing me out of my thoughts and back to reality.

As we land I give a mocking bow with a dismissive gesture towards the ocean recanting .

"Welcome to the Ocean, a place of Majesty and Beauty, please enjoy your stay while we can still accommodate you."

My sarcasm hits its mark perfectly, making her laugh pleasantly as her gaze drifted off to scan the oceans waves.

"It really is a sight, huh?" I say. coming to stand next to her.

"We used to come here every summer until They showed up." My voice turns icy at the unwelcome memories of dreary weather, small cells and daily contests, most lasting to the death.

Noticing shudders running over her body, I mentally slap myself.

"Don't worry about it. I didn't mean to include you in that flash back, sorry."

She shakes her head slowly, tears glinting in her eyes.

"It's fine, at least I learned something of your past with your consent." She laughed brokenly, and I cringe inwardly for bringing this upon her.

"Hey, think happy." I whisper softly, brushing my lips against her exposed neck and shifting my gaze towards the blue moon hanging suspended in the sky.

She takes the hint immediately and takes off just after I see the rising colour flood her cheeks.

She flew straight into the eye of the moon, looking more like an indistinct silhouette than a living angel.

The moon's eerie glow caught even the smallest imperfections in her frame, sending stray stands of hair glowing white and outlining her frame with a precision that even outdid the best realistic artists in all the angel kingdoms.

At first I didn't notice it but as she proceeded further into the ceremony I felt an unseen force grip me, its gentle fingers grasping and slipping only to grasp again, the moon's light rays bent and surged of their own accord, beaconing towards it…and her.

Her eyes were closed and a watery sphere of shining and sparkling salt water rose and swelled around her but it only half closed, leaving space for me to fly into it as well and with a final tug the spun moon beams succeeded in driving me into the air and directing me towards Myra, and the moon's glowing eye, which seemed to grow brighter the closer I got to it.

It took me a while to understand what had happened; it was so bright in the water sphere.

"The Gift…" a rustling voice whispered, coming and going at the wind's call though I was almost positive it was the moon who was speaking.

"The Gift." it said, more demanding this time, and then it hit me why I was there—the link.

How could I have forgotten, the moon must think I'm a part of her.

"No, we don't." The voice was fainter this time, singing rather than speaking. "We know who you are Rick, and you are meant to receive this gift. You are special too."

This froze my thoughts and my body. I don't even know how I kept my wing beats steady.

"You were so young, you wouldn't remember."

Now they had my attention and my curiosity.

"What do you mean, who are you?" I asked, half afraid of the answer.

"Remember your lessons of the Golden Gateway little prince, your blood runs deep, as does that of your sisters'. I'm glad they are still pure ones, and how I wish you had bought them with you to us." The voice sighed wistfully, now I was just plain confused.

"What sisters?" I asked, full of defence.

"Why, we speak of your older sister Silvia and the half-year twins Rose and Misty, though they don't act alike in any way whatsoever, and," the voice stopped itself before the next words were uttered, "here is our riddle for you and your power. I sting and bite, I'm hard to control and enjoy the company of lightning, and dry wood, what am I?"

The answer was simple and jumped to my head immediately.

'Fire.'

I thought, and there it was, flickering over my skin, it was everywhere…but it didn't hurt. It seemed to heal and relish my company more than ever.

"Its name is Dream. She heals as easily as she hurts. Know how and where to use her and you will be fine.

She is a family heirloom so treat her well and you may be surprised at how well you get along with her, and how well your siblings get along with her sisters."

The voice seemed to change, turning into the lapping ebb and flow of the waves and then I saw Myra still in the sphere and the moon's final words echoed over the sea,

"Heed these words… know the Spirit, know the person.

Read them as you would read a good book, care for them as you would a child and listen to them as you would a friend…"

And then they were gone, five spheres of pure spun light that disappeared into the moon's eye.

In a blinding flash Myra seemed to glide over the water and collapse onto a close-by sand dune…

CHAPTER 21: RICK - THE PRICE OF POWER

Beaten and bruised, I wake up to find Myra still sleeping on the nearby dune. Then, like a rush of flaming fire,

I remember my conversation with the moon spirit and,

my new power...

'Prince..?' I think sardonically. If so I wasn't a very good one,

and yet still I wondered...

Flashes of strawberry blonde, orange, red, hungry, devouring flames and worst of all those terrified screams.

Then a realization hit me,

I can see the past... and that's when it happened.

Suddenly I wasn't standing on the northern beaches anymore. I was in a castle-like foyer, dark blue banners with a crescent moon resting in a full sun hung all around the room and then there was a table filled with all manner of delicacies.

It looked like they were on the main course. They, being a man with brown hair and blue eyes and a sweet young woman with hair like watery fire and eyes of chocolaty intelligence. As I turned to look behind me, I gasp as tears hot and hurried pricked and ran from my eyes and down my cheeks.

I'd seen Rose as a baby, but she wasn't playing with me as we'd been told as kids, she was playing with a girl of about ten years of age and with her reflection.

No, not her reflection, her twin.

"Misty..." I whispered, testing the name on my tongue. It sounded very familiar, and then I scanned to my left and saw myself.

I was three, so cute and innocent and I was already hovering! Another person entered the foyer at the edge of my vision...

A sharp slap on my legs brought me back to reality and I wake up lying face-up drenched in salt water up to my chest. Shivering slightly, I see Myra sitting next to me, watching the water with a crystal clear expression.

Shifting her position towards me, she starts before smiling at me; her gaze kept flicking towards the sea...

A frown creased my forehead as I tried to figure out why she was acting like this; she seemed totally immune to the things going on around her, as if she was cut off from her physical body.

Her smile wavers and then outright disappears as she notices the frown resting on my brow.

Everything seems to spin and swim before my eyes and then I see her.

"Silvia..?" My voice sounds different, younger and higher than normal...

She was standing on a golden balcony. Bird song rippled over us though the tension in her stance remained.

She wore a dress of fine silk coloured every hue of blue with silver gems. Her hair was a sandy blonde running down her back in gentle waves but the tips were a reddish copper. Her wings were folded neatly against her back, shining brightly in the moonlight. They were crisp white and only started to turn honeyed gold as they reached the very tips.

She started at my intrusion into her thoughts and smiled down at me through long, pale eyelashes.

"You must hurry!" she whispered to me urgently.

"Leave before it's too late!"

Only then did I realize what had happened to my kingdom,

"Who did this!"

My eyes flashed dangerously and seemed to hurt Silvia more than my words.

"Please Rick, think of others over yourself." she pleaded and then she was fading becoming indistinct and drifting away,

forgotten.

Pounding footsteps, the smell of burnt wood and fabric, the soft cry of Rose as I snatch her away from Misty and run.

The screams of my people echoing behind me.

The jeering of the bandits who destroyed my home and worst of all…the figure falling from the balcony, trailing ribbons of blood from her body.

"Noooo!!!" The mental scream bought me back to reality and I found Myra sitting next to me, ridged and still.

Her eyes had glazed over and tears rolled freely down her face. Myra and I were physically, mentally and magically opposed to one another.

From Dream to Nightmare.

I shudder, chilled.

What now?

The question had polluted my thinking for the last few hours. One thing was clear, the moon spirits had given me a task, one that involved the guarded secret of the institution. It was one I couldn't complete by myself, yet Myra was hesitant to leave.

What troubles her so that she cannot leave, let alone tell me, but make herself suffer so!

As my anger faded a simple, fearful explanation presents itself. She's afraid…

I almost laughed at the idea of Myra being scared, but of late she'd been acting differently than she usually would.

'I don't know what to do!'

Her thoughts crashed into my mind, sending me to my knees as I struggled not to cry out in pain.

Who's she talking to? And more importantly, why?

Still Myra spoke, growing weaker and more agitated with every counter-sentence obviously thrown at her.

'Why should I return home!?' Myra was literally pleading now. 'What good would it do us?' she pressing agitation and getting closer to anger.

All of a sudden I was able to hear the full conversation, and the recipient of the information was none other than,

Flera Flame the queen of 'The Golden Gateway' fallen kingdom, also known as my mother.

'I need you to lead him there, only then can he return home and regain control of the kingdom.'

Her voice projected years of experience, gained wisdom and still growing beauty.

'Rick isn't a prince, let alone one from that fallen kingdom!' Myra spoke then and Queen Flera had already prepared a counter sentence.

'His sister's names are Rose and Misty. They are the half-year twins and only when they are together will their powers merge to reach a higher level of power and connection.

His older sister's name was Silvia, not even I know where she is or what happened to her that night...' Flera's voice saddened as her memory triggered images of Silvia.

She doesn't know..?

Hope flooded my soul at the possibility that Silvia was still alive, banishing any shadowing doubts from my mind, unfortunately revealing my presence to both Flera and Myra.

'Flera?' I asked cautiously, afraid of the answer and of her reaction to the question that had just dawned on me.

'Where's Rose now?'

The woman's mask slipped at my direct question and her eyes saddened with the memory of the conversation with Jade and her daughter.

'They are prisoners of Prince Aqua. They are tortured every day for your location and no-one believes them when they tell the truth. You must hurry if you want to save them before their demise.' She spoke the truth bluntly, making it all the more painful to hear.

'We 'll leave at dawn.' I say curtly, eyes burning at the mention of, Rose, and, torture, put together.

I barely noticed Myra's sad glance in my direction; my emotions were roiling, burning and churning together. It took all of my self control to remain calm and contained in my state. And then it began to disappear, flowing out of me in waves of anger and frustration and only then did I notice the glow in the east emanating from Dawn herself and in the west her brother.

Dusk dulled the surrounding landscape, trying and not succeeding in blotting out his sister's light to bring on the coming night.

"Wait… Why would Prince Aqua want them? Of what use are they to him?" Myra spoke boldly, voicing everyone's hidden hopes and doubts.

"He wants the 'Duel Power' for himself, and for that he needs all five opposites of the three dimensions, three pairs from the Angel World, one from the human's world and one from Mermaid's Reef. You all know Prince Aqua has access to the Mermaid's Realm and he has a way of forcing us to give him Misty, Myra, Rick, Dawn and Dusk." Everyone grew quiet in speculation when the two true reasons were presented to me.

"He wants me to locate and capture the remaining human twins and then he'll use all our combined powers to rule the three Realms, four, if you include the Lair of the Demons." The statement hit its mark and everyone froze, deep in thought trying to devise a plan to end this madness sought after by so many.

'The Institution wasn't far off in their speculation of Myra, she really is special, but she isn't the only one…' I think and then I see the same thought cross Myra's face as it did mine.

"It's totally insane…"

Myra starts slowly,

"but what if we could half our twin selves?"

I pick up her line,

"and only go there in halves, saving our loved ones and keeping the world at peace…mostly, anyways."

Myra flashes a smile in my direction, which I return in kind and this time Flera catches our meaning.

'You mean to split the opposites, twins, whatever off from each other?'

She understood the predicament perfectly.

'You do know one without the other will perish together, right?' She thinks, speaking through the mental link she'd established with all of us present when first forming the connection. She surprises us with her knowledge of opposites.

"Only if they stay apart for more than one lunar cycle (two weeks) and they seem to survive perfectly well when they don't yet know each other." I point out, speaking aloud, since I'm well aware that Flera can hear us, even if she chooses not to speak verbally for now.

"Yes but you will grow weaker with each day that you are apart now that you have met; how do you expect to locate and manage to get to your opposite in time, before you die?"

Flera asked, growing fearful for her only son.

"We'll discuss the matter in the morning, until then, perhaps it would be wise to decide which half will go and which will stay and wait?"

Myra concluded our discussion briskly before retiring to sit next to me. Before she had a chance to speak I stated my position without so much as a hitch, knowing she'd try to argue with me the instant my words sunk in.

"I'll go free the others, stay here and help us however you can, but do not, under any circumstances, come find me."

She stiffens at my hard voice, then her own demeanour hardened profusely.

"I will not let Melody suffer in such circumstances while I sit here as if on vacation!" she hissed through gritted teeth.

"Well, I won't let you get hurt and I have more reason to go since my sister and Storm are in danger."

That argument silenced both of us.

It was decided…

The real struggle would be met when morning came, so, for the time being, I decided to catch up on some sleep.

We'd see what the morrow would bring when it came.

CHAPTER 22: MYRELLE - SPIRITUAL EMBERS

After Dusk managed to quench Dawn's light enough to bring forth the night, Flera vanished from our minds and all was peaceful that night while everyone slept.

The next morning brought with it much discussion emanating from each pair of opposites. We were only two, Dawn and Dusk, and Myra and me.

Reasoning was the best and most used option to win the debate of go and stay.

Since Rick and I had already concluded our debate last night, we were free to help the other opposite pair gain one side of the argument.

In the end the results were that Rick and Dusk would go since it was considered too risky to allow Misty to accompany them in spirit when her opposite was at their destination (Rose).

It didn't help that we were almost clueless about the other two opposites, both of which would bring huge political issues to light, should we have need of either of them.

The humans spoke for themselves. Should something happen to their young ones they would seek us out with the fire of revenge in their eyes.

The mermaids were a stern, strong and suspicious race, thinking of their own interests and safety before anything or anyone else's, but they just so happened to be ruled by a certain Prince Aqua.

'Any tactical decisions to be made?'

Rick's thoughts brushed mine; shocking me out of my mind's eye, back to reality.

"Obviously." I state audibly, rolling my eyes at him.

"How do we know where to look?" Rick asked me, wasting no breath explaining our predicament.

"You don't" I answer before letting a sly smile ease his concern. "...but I do."

"You know it's too dangerous for you to accompany us." he said, eyes flashing.

"I didn't say anything about physical presence." I shoot back quickly, smiling as he finally understands my intent.

~

Until that moment when Myra suggested it, I'd never fully understood the power our mental connection gave us.

It seemed to open up a whole new level of trust, intimacy and power.

Sure enough as soon as I'd understood our mental connection, the moon spirits came and altered day to night even though it was supposed to be ten in the morning.

At their presence none of us noticed Dawn's form waver dangerously.

The moon spirits surrounded us, chattering excitedly and then a single voice made the others fall silent.

"You've done well. But now you will be tested. Tread cautiously, for the ground on which you walk is unstable and harsh. Your tool for success is to have Faith."

The moon spirits started to fade but then they noticed Dawn. That's when they shimmered, turning from their usual pale blue to white to yellow to orange to an angry red and advancing towards her at a quickening pace.

When they reached her, she sang and flew, and they followed, like a shadow she couldn't get rid of.

When she paused to catch her breath they pounced, holding her in place.

One of the spirits took the form of a rainbow lorikeet letting all the colour drip from its feathers. A rainbow pool formed at its feet and a shadow bird stood in the place of the once beautiful animal.

The other spirits buzzed excitedly, calling Dawn all sorts of names; light stealer, colour bringer, and death's pet were all names spat at the poor bird.

When the shadow bird lifted her head and plunged its beak towards dawn's exposed breast, a different song split the silence, causing the shadow bird to miss her mark and instead her beak sank into Dawn's wing.

The piercing screech of pain that came from Dawn made all the moon spirits chatter happily, enjoying her pain. Meanwhile the shadow bird turned to face an angry Dusk. "My child." the moon spirit whispered brokenly, seeing her son at last.

"What do you want, Luna!?" Dusk asked, he was irritated,
and far beyond reasoning.

"My son." Luna answered.

"I know him not." Dusk replied, breaking the spirit's heart.

"Leave, and don't you dare hurt my sister again, ever!"

Luna's own anger flared as she thought, 'How could he remember his sister and not his own mother!' But when he flew down to Dawn and sang in lament over her, the spirits retreated with a shocked leader.

Dawn was in far worse condition than anyone else.

Her wing had a pecked hole in it and the shadow birds' poison was spreading through her body quickly, dulling her splendour and colour.

"Where is father? I cannot see him yet I know he must be here."

Dawn's voice rasped weakly, but the truth in her words struck everyone. Why hadn't the sun come back?

"That's your job, remember? You sing to the plants and animals, calling forth the sun and the light, banishing all shadow."

'That explains Luna's aimed anger at her...'

The thought crossed both Myra's and my own mind at the same time.

Another idea presented itself to me.

"Dusk? Can Myra help?"

If she could just heal the wound, I could take care of the rest.

'Her power isn't strong enough to heal such a wound.' The bird shook his head sadly.

"We'll try anyway." I growl.

I don't know what it was, maybe the fact that I said we,

but Dusk let Myra and I go to Dawn. Together we knelt before the injured little bird, such a small being holding such a large amount of love and power.

"We'll help you." Myra whispered softly, comforting her.

Myra spread her wings in preparation for the healing, wanting to capture as much water as she could from the air before beginning.

"You mind if I go first?" I ask.

Even though she was confused, she indicated her approval. 'Dream, I need your help!' She heard and she appeared causing both Dusk and Myra to gasp.

The flame was warm and dangerous.

"Heal." I whisper, letting my breath wash over the flames lulling them into the state of blue heat and intensity used to heal.

"Another secret, Rick?" Myra whispered questioningly.

"Your turn." I grin at her.

In response she rolled her eyes and takes to the sky.

A few minutes later Myra returns full of cloud dew and warm sunlight. She begins the healing completion of Dawn.

At first her eyes flutter, then they open wide and tears prick her and Dusk's eyes as they silently rejoice at her renewed life force. Testing her wings, Dusk accompanies Dawn on a little review flight in the morning's rays.

"How did you manage to get Dream's power?" Myra asked, letting her mask slip to reveal her bewilderment.

"Don't trust anyone you don't know, but heed any advice, wherever it may come from," I answer with a riddle of my own, knowing Myra would understand it within the hour.

"I'll heed that advice as well."

She smirked, having already figured out what I meant.

~

His eyes brightened at the quickness of my response,

but that wasn't the only reason they brightened. An idea had flashed in his mind.

"We could intensify the strength of our mental link through a spiritual connection allowing us to see each other's spirit..."

Rick started.

"And that would establish a spiritual connection allowing us to see and use the others' senses." I finish, astonished at the simplicity of the matter.

"Lets get started then… Myra, if you would?"

It was more a statement than a question but I hooked onto his humour anyway.

"Of course…" I smile at him dramatically, making him laugh.

"Ok, try to relax and lower your conscious barriers." I breathe quietly, and then I see him…

Not him exactly, more his spiritual energy form, and I sense that he can see mine too.

His is coloured darker shades on account of his impureness but flecks of white and gold can be seen in his shimmering form.

'What?

But that means…'

CHAPTER 23: MYRELLE - QUESTIONS UNANSWERED

'Rick's a Royal?'

Confused, but unwilling to forgo the opportunity, I study his spirit, intently noting the high amount of Gold and the bright white flecks that appeared inconsistently.

His Aura mainly consisted of various shades of blue and a lavender purple.

Shades of dusky orange and pink flashed about rarely and a single fleck of unwavering red replaced his heart, beating as any heart would.

'What do all these colours mean?' I wonder and the thought bounces right back at me. It's not my thought though,

its Ricks.

"You look like a blazing rainbow framed in gold. Your core is Gold too." he says, noting his observations so that I can understand myself better.

"You look like dusk at the ocean. Your core is a bright pulsing red."

Slowly our surroundings started to shift, merge and change.

Now we weren't standing on a grey plain but in a room full of mirrors.

Each mirror reflected our spirits in a different way, showing tints of colours unseen before due to our inability to see many other angles of our spiritual bodies.

Rick's spirit also included five silver white flecks hovering around his core, basically encircling him.

Seeing my own reflection, I notice the absence of the yellow colour as normally seen in a rainbow.

I have those silver flecks as well, but mine were only three in quantity.

A nagging suspicion came to mind that the colours weren't the only things we didn't understand, and the acknowledgment Rick sent me only broadened those possibilities.

"What do you suppose the colours, space and quantities represent?" I ask, curious.

"Something tells me we're about to find out." Rick replied grimly, and sure enough, the landscape was shifting once more.

Black.

That's all you can see,

Pitch black.

Like a tranquil pool unaffected by the ravages of time around it, a blurred reflection appears at its centre and soon I can see the form of a flower starting to bud and bloom.

On the outside it was a dark yet vibrant blue and as its features materialized and became more distinct, its petals rustled open to reveal teal flecks on the inner circle of stark white.

The tips of the petals were the same colour as the outside of the flower, but what had gone unnoticed before slipped into both Rick's and my view, showing the faint dusting of silver along the edges of the petals. As the flower surfaced from that inky black pool and its dusky pink pollen dried instantly and blew about the pond, settling on Rick and Myra, they returned to their physical selves.

"Well that was definitely worth it." I piped.

"Indeed, and it seems my little friend has come up with a purpose and a name for herself…" Rick wondered.

'Stardusk…' sang the silken voice before leaving.

A single snowflake drifted from the sky and fell onto the tip of my nose, sending a cold chill up my spine.

Looking up at the sky, I notice snow clouds hovering above us, thickly blocking out the sun's warming rays.

"The first day of winter." I say, chilled.

"The Day of the Mist." he clarifies and his eyes clear, as he understands.

"Happy Birthday Misty." we both whisper into the wind, and as we turn away a single ray of sunlight breaks the cloud cover.

Dawn and Dusk look at us and then I realize it isn't morning but late afternoon.

'They're already behind time and the weather isn't about to help them.' I think grimly.

"Good Luck, and come back safely." I wish them.

"I'll bring them back, I promise." Rick reassures me.

"Don't make promises you can't keep, Rick." I whisper before flying away.

I couldn't stand parting with him and the tears had already started to stream down my face before I could leave him.

~

Her declaration left me unsettled since I could well remember
the time when I'd said the same to her.

She'd kept her promise, though it cost her and Melody dearly.

Focusing on the flight ahead, I mutter a quick goodbye to Dawn and follow Dusk into the sky.

Later, just as Myra had feared, the weather sprung up with a snowstorm.

The only positive thing was that the wind was at our backs and that's when Dusk makes a dive for the ground, quickly followed by me thanks to my tracker training.

We land, and I'm waist deep in the snow.

"What's up?" I ask, trying to lighten his mood.

It doesn't work.

"It seems the little prince is aware of our course." Dawn replies bluntly.

"What!?" I say, shocked.

"His wind and water friends have informed him of our course and he's trying to exhaust us, at this rate we would have been there faster. But," he continues warningly, "we would've been there early in the morning and we need to sleep to keep on top of things, so I suggest you rake out a cavern for us from your waist down and we'll start up again in the morning."

I do as he bids, because he's so straightforward and seems to know more about the little prince than even Myra and I do.

"So, tell me, how many of our creations do you actually know?" Dusk asked with surprising intensity for our situation.

"I know of the Blue Jay, Opal. That's all."

This made Dusk chuckle before answering with a mind whirling riddle.

"I said our 'Creations' did I not?" he restated.

"Well, yes, but what does the word, Creation, have to do with your work?" I ask. I was totally confuzzled.

"Absolutely everything." Dusk states and promptly tucks his head under his wing and goes to sleep, leaving me to mull over my cluttered thoughts alone.

It's early morning.

I can tell by the way my breath fogs up before me and how the light shining through the snow is white, indicating moonlight.

Dusk's gone.

That worries me but not enough that I go look for him.

I do, however, get up and shake the snow from my clothes before stretching the aches and pains out of my body.

I'm gazing longingly at the moon when a voice enters my thoughts:

'Miss you too.' says Myra.

I smile sadly at her tone. Her voice brings back a pang of guilt at leaving her, but I quickly push it aside.

I'd learned not to dwell on these things the hard way and I'm not about restart a bad habit.

With a rush of wind and streaks of blue, black, purple and pink, Dusk lands before me, eyes blazing like heated coals. "He's decided to try and intercept our rescue with force.

We'd better get a move on if we want to stay ahead of them." Dusk puffs out in one breath.

I'm on my feet in seconds, wings half spread to take off when I notice Dusk still on the ground, looking at me expectantly. "What?" I snap, irritated.

He seems to snap out of his trance.

"Just curious," he says and then rouses himself. "What are you looking at?" he asked and then brushes past me as if nothing happened.

Shrugging off my uneasy feeling, I follow him into the sky just as the sun starts to rise behind us.

"Looks like she can't prolong it any longer. I should've left earlier."

Dusk chastises so quietly I barely caught onto his stream of words.

'Of course', I think to myself. That would explain why I felt so awake and why Dusk looked so worn when he came back.

I pull together the puzzle pieces so easily I can't believe I hadn't thought of the idea myself.

'Don't lose your focus now Rick.'

I knew the warning was coming long before the thought intrudes my mind.

'Don't waste your energy now, Myra.' I throw back and she severs the connection almost immediately.

Focusing on the task at hand, I barely have time to manoeuvre when Dusk calls out, 'Watch it, Rick'

I miss the rock jutting out of the Ocean by a hairs breadth,

and I'm almost positive I heard a half snort half chuckle come from Myra's direction, making me smile too.

Dusk catches on long before I do.

'Don't touch those rocks.' he warns. 'They're an alarm system designed by the little prince's elite guard.'

That was alarming considering the fact that the elite guard of the Prince of the Sea and Sky were a combination of Pure Breed Angels and the finest warriors of the sea, the mermaids.

Compelled by fear for the second time in my life, I dodge with increasing speed wanting to get to the end of this trap set as fast as possible.

Without warning the water darkened and the traps ceased. 'That, is where we'll find our friends.' Dusk confirms startling me, and sure enough,

rising out of the sea was a prison-like structure made out of sea boulders, reinforced with the rare sea earth that no magic could penetrate.

'Now would be a good time to contact Myra.' Dusk says grimly.

'I think we'd better land on those rocks first and then enter

from the side, seeing as how the main entries would be made for creations of the sea and sky.' I suggest, already moving towards the cluster of boulders. Before the bird can reply, and before I've even touched the rocks, a strangled half cry half whimper escapes Dusk's throat and his wings stop working.

In a single swift motion I catch the falling bird and zigzag the trap course in record time, returning the bird to the beach.

"What was that!?" I ask angrily.

I don't get an answer.

"Ok, then tell me how to get in there." I say, exasperatedly.

"Why, on earth would you want to go into that place?"

came an amused answer and as I turn around I catch my first glimpse of Prince Aqua.

"You might want to reconsider that."

the Prince says, interpreting my stance and emotion.

"After all, you did want to bring them back alive… right?"

he chuckles and there above him are Storm, Melody and Rose all being held in a water wind based cage!

CHAPTER 24: RICK - DUSTED GOLD

Knowing that my friends were captured was totally different to actually experiencing the heart wrenching pain of seeing them locked up.

Hot anger seared through my veins, only succeeding in sharpening my focus.

With a loud cry I spring on the Prince, catching everyone by surprise.

I'd always been taught never to underestimate my opponent but the same was also true in reverse and the Prince seemed to have forgotten that.

Indeed I was able to pin the Prince down before leaning in and hissing, "If anything happens to my sister it's on your head."

Then I back away and make my way to the cages and examine them from all angles. A sad shake from Melody indicated that it's infused with some sort of magic repellent as well.

Rose seems overjoyed to see me and that lightened my mood as well. Unfortunately the prince took advantage of my distraction to call his nephew.

'Wow, that kid's hot.'

And if Myra thought so, the possibility that Rose would fall for him was more than high enough to be concerning.

Sending a mental message to Storm, I think as loudly as I can manage 'Block Rose's view!'

He may not have heard me but he certainly recognized the danger.

The kid looked to be about Rose's age, maybe a year or so older.

Chocolate hair, caramel eyes tinted with hazel, reflecting flecks of gold and silver, tanned features and he looked extremely lithe, agile and fast.

'Great. I have to deal with him too.' I think bitterly.

'You do realize what those colours mean, right?' Myra says, noting his Spirit Aura.

'Yeah, he's royal and still pure. Thanks for the reminder.'

I send her the thought and try to focus, but then something catches my eye. The kid was wearing a petite looking crown.

'What a find…for a guy.' I think before I see the emblem engraved on the front.

It was the goldfinch in flight and in its eye was a gem that gleamed like emerald fire in the sun.

'Could it be chance?'

I muse, seeing Rose's eyes gleam green in the evening light, reflecting the crown.

"Where'd you get that crown, little prince?" I ask him mockingly. All the while never taking my eyes off the boy.

That wrings a dry smile out of him.

"We stole it from the treasure keep of the Golden Kingdom, ever heard of it?"

he asks in an equally mocking tone, but I'm not listening anymore, because resting on his head is a crown of similar make with a thicker band but this time the eye has a goldish brown zircon gem in it.

I can feel my eyes film over.

I can see the brown reflection they're creating before me.

"We were able to save all of them." the prince drawls on. "The eye colour still confuses me though…"

He was talking about the crowns belonging to Misty and Silvia!

"The others have the gems…" the Prince begins.

"Apatite and Agate." I finish, already knowing the gems that most resemble my sister's eyes best.

"How'd you know that?"

The prince is suspicious now, verging on scared, and there's nothing more dangerous than a person with power who's frightened.

"You forgot the other two." the Prince continues, trying to regain his composure.

"You mean the crowns of the King and Queen?"

The Princes eyes flashed, wrong answer apparently.

"Those gems would be Azurite and Moonstone."

I remember my mothers eye colour instinctively and I knew my father somehow became blind and the crown would have been altered accordingly.

I actually saw the colour drain from his face.

"Who are you?"

he hisses.

"How can you know these things, that even I didn't figure out until after I had the crowns examined?"

His voice is dangerously low. I know he's seconds from mentally losing it, but I have a bigger problem now.

Somehow Rose has managed to catch a glimpse of me and the boy. What's worse, she seems to be trying to use her power to free the others.

I'm running out of time and energy.

An idea, careless but possible, settles in my mind.

I haven't used my natural power yet but I have a feeling it has an elemental quality if I can just utilize it enough to free the others the mission would be half way finished.

There is however, still the issue of keeping the boy distracted long enough for me to gather my remaining strength.

The boy keeps glancing sideways and I realize he's trying to catch a glimpse of Rose.

A flash of her red hair makes him turn an inch further in her direction.

'Clever girl.' I think.

She's given me just the opportunity I needed.

With no hesitation I begin exercising my natural gift, feeling the earth, trees, rocks, air and water around me. Then,

I lock onto the cages and begin the tedious task of devising the construction of the cages and so learning the way to

disassemble them.

With no warning at all the cages disperse.

Rose, Melody and Storm come to my aid immediately.

Rose flashes me a smile and I realize what happened.

"He likes you, doesn't he?" I ask, finally understanding.

"Yep, he's been trying to see me head to toe ever since the Prince captured us." she answers shining with happiness at being with me again.

"Now he can have the honour of seeing you in action." I say.

"See that crown on his head? Get that and put it on your own, you'll understand why later." I explain.

She raises her eyebrow at me but does as I bid anyway.

"His name is Daniel."

she calls over her shoulder.

"I'm going for the Prince. He won't underestimate me again so I could use some help." I say dismissively.

Storm takes my invitation without complaint.

"Melody, see if you can help Dusk." I call to her.

The Prince had since retreated somewhat after I'd been able to tell him all the gems in each of the crowns of the Golden Kingdom.

A couple of boulders separated us from him. We crossed them easily only to find the little weakling surrounded by his elite guard in the shallows of the sea.

A sinister quirk of his lips tells me he's given them the allowance to kill.

With the fastest reflexes I'd ever seen, Storm overshadows the guards, dives in and pulls up just in time before the guards raise their weapons against him.

He'd managed to give me an opening however, and I wasn't about to let that chance slip away.

Gliding down on silent wings, I grip the crown and rip it from his head and before anyone can react Melody and Dusk are attacking as well.

"Good to have you back!" I shout into the wind happily.

Then the realization hits me.

Wind…

Sure enough the waves are churning in the storm as well and the Prince's face is mottled with rage.

Setting the crown on my head, I turn around to find Rose and Daniel being tossed in the wind like leaves.

Flight definitely wasn't an option, but maybe I could try Myra's trick.

Centring all my thoughts on the life around me I call upon
the power of natural elements once again forming a wind protective
barrier around both Rose and Daniel and bring them down to the ground
again. Having Rose by my side again relived me massively.

'I'm beginning to understand why you put yourself through all that pain
now.' I think in Myra's direction, remembering all the times she'd fainted
from the exertion of her strength and powers.

Then I notice something else.

"You couldn't get it, could you?" I ask patiently.

"No, he's just too enduring." she says sadly.

"We'll see how he fairs against me then, huh?"

I smile at her and take off the air and water once again, clear and calm.

"Daniel." I say announcing my appearance and challenge.

"Just hand over the crown already." I say trying to sound irritated and
impatient.

"Not a chance." he sneers at me.

I'll tell you this kid's got guts, challenging me.

He takes off and lands a fist on my cheek before I even have time to
retaliate.

"Fine, you wanna play? Lets play." I sneer back at him.

Seems he thought I'd give up after the first encounter, must run in the
family how they always underestimate their opponents.

Now the fun really began: I kick and punch, catching him in the
shoulder and stomach.

After that I loop around and clamp his wings together struggling to
resist the temptation of letting go at all,

we hit the ground hard, he gets the brunt of it though.

With a quick twist I free my arms from under him and grab the crown
on his head before he can even begin to think clearly again.

"Ok, here's the deal." I state, explaining our predicament to Rose.
"Mum and Dad aren't our real parents, and you have two siblings other
than me." Her eyes widen as I continue. "You're one of the Princesses of
the Golden Kingdom, and Mum and Dad were actually the King and
Queen, so, the rulers of that kingdom." I finish dismissively.

It takes a few seconds for her to process this, then, "Who were our
other siblings?" she asks almost shyly.

"We'll discuss it later, I promise you that, but right now we really need
to leave here."

She accepts my evasion indifferently and we get back to the others in a
matter of minutes, but when we see our camp, we freeze.

Dusk's call of lament runs over the earth as plants and animals curl up,
defenceless against his pain, loss and rage.

"Let's take a look around, we might find something or someone." I say, trying to stay in control of my roiling emotions. Everyone looks everywhere but we all come back empty handed.

Then, the smallest shiver of leaves in the tree right above us.

And from that tree Dawn bursts forth totally infuriated.

She looked about ready to rip a tree out by the roots and throw it halfway around the Angel world.

'Dawn!' Dusk's voice brings me back to reality.

"Where's Myra?" I ask, concerned.

At the mention of Myra, Dawn tenses up again.

'They… They came out of nowhere, we both fought them off but when one of them caught me by the wing she said she'd come quietly if they let me go. They complied, but didn't hold the full bargain, they came back again looking for me, undoubtedly.'

She almost finished her tale but I already knew the rest, so I took over for her, 'So you hid in that tree until they left. They tried to get your attention though multiple offenses against everything you stand for but you held firm in your resolve.'

She seemed surprised that I'd been able to discern so much from the way she looked. That was the reason Dusk had fainted.

He would have had to made contact with the sea earth for it to affect him that much, and now these thugs had Myra.

'I ripped this from his tunic, it might mean something but I'm not quite sure what.' she chirped mentally, revealing a russet piece of cloth with a golden seal embroidered into it.

The seal was a set of angels wings caught in a single cloud, "That's the seal of Angel Heaven!" I exclaim, before the fact dawns on me.

"Raise your hand or wing if you know Myra's real name." Dawn's and Dusk's wings shoot up and so did Melody's and Storm's. Not counting me meant that the only person who didn't know Myra's real name was Rose.

"Have any of you ever said this name out loud, or even thought it?" I ask urgently. Everyone shakes their heads.

"There must be something one of us did otherwise they wouldn't have been able to track her and finally the message sinks in.

"You mean, they found her because her name was uttered?" Dawn was absolutely devastated.

It dawned on e then.

"Flera," I growl then sigh. I should've known.

Myra's vision seemed to be coming true after all, and all I could remember was the jeering of her people, the blood that spilled around me and Misty laying on those steps wounded almost beyond recognition.

"I think it'd be best if we settle in for the night, we've got plans to make tomorrow." I say, already distancing myself from the others.

'Why didn't she warn me? Why didn't she do something to alert us?'

I ask myself and, as usual, I don't receive an answer.

Morning comes much too quickly for all of us. We're still tired as Dawn begins to raise the already late sun to signal the morning.

Dew clings to every surface, glistening and glinting in the rising sun.

A few clouds drift aimlessly through the sky. Funny how nature can interpret your feelings so easily.

We had bigger problems than the weather though.

'How are we supposed to get her back!?' I think helplessly.

I knew it was too good to be true, I knew she wouldn't be able to stay with us forever and still I'd hoped.

My thoughts turn sad and bitter.

The alarm call of a goldfinch snaps me back to myself and out of my depressing thoughts.

Wait a sec… why would a bird be giving an alarm call? There are absolutely no dangers around here.

Unless… Dawn.

They were coming back for Dawn, and what a surprise they received when they stumbled into our camp.

Because of our presence and numbers it didn't surprise me when they started to retreat, fear already spreading through their expressions.

They didn't get the chance to run before we cornered them against the very same boulder that I now saw had streaks of dried blood on its lower surface.

That did it.

In all my years as a seeker I'd never lost my composure.

I guess there's always a first time for everything, and, in all honesty, it felt good to vent all my frustration.

By the time I'd finished with them their bodies were already turning black and blue.

They'd fainted after the first few impacts hit them so at least I knew I hadn't killed anyone.

I knew what they'd wanted, I knew who they'd come to retrieve,

and I knew who they were, but, one question was still unanswered:

Why did they come back, again?

CHAPTER 25: MYRELLE - THE SAPPHIRE SHINES

Prisoner.

I was a prisoner again, in my own house.

Sure I could move around the palace, but the windows are barred, the doors barricaded and guarded.

There wasn't even the slightest shift in the air, not a breeze stirred in the Palace.

'Welcome home Myrelle.' I think bitterly.

Although here everyone referred to me as Princess Sapphire, as was only proper of them.

Them being the lords and ladies who passed me in the corridors.

The last few days had been spent mostly relearning and polishing up my manners and political speech etiquette,

so that I could participate in the political small talk conversations held at the dinner feast that had been going on in my favor ever since I'd been recaptured, because that's exactly what it felt like.

I'd had the smallest taste of freedom and all the feelings that came with it only to be pulled right back into the cage where I'd started off.

Ok, I wont deny it, I miss them, Melody and Rick especially.

I wish I could've spent more time with all of them,

but fate, apparently, had other ideas.

Unwillingly, I remember the vision I'd shared with Rick.

Was it even possible?

Could someone like him really commit such an unforgivable sin that he was to be thrown in the arena to compete against our finest sportsmen?

What's more, who? Who in the world could possibly want to hurt him that much? I couldn't dwell on my lost life now;

I was about to be thrown into my own worst nightmare too.

I hadn't seen my parents since they'd sent me away to that school, which was about three years ago. Their little budding rose had bloomed and withered only to bud once more three times round since they'd last set eyes on me.

You could tell my mother was absolutely relieved to know I was safe; she was also amazed at how much I'd changed over the course of three years.

My father was a whole other story. He looked furious, and that's putting it lightly.

You could see that tiny flicker of admiration for my survival and his posture told me he was slightly impressed with my frame.

"I'm so glad you're home," my mother says with a sad smile, her eyes shining with misty tears.

"How do you find your accommodations?" my father asks breezily.

Leave it to my dad to treat everyone the same. Still he wrings a tight, uneasy smile out of me.

"How have you been fairing since last we spoke?" my mother asks gently.

"Well enough, we graduated from the Institution a year or so earlier." A common answer tinged with sarcasm,

Rule 7: always add a bit of sarcasm to your answer.

My parents seemed pleased enough by it anyway.

"What's this really about?"

I've always been the type of person to get straight to the point, it's one of the traits I gained from my father.

"Well, if you must know..." I was already concerned by his tone, "...our country is suffering from disobedient citizens. Our Law seems to have multiple flaws in it that have gone unnoticed for quite some time and we mean to patch up those holes."

He paused for breath.

"Preferably, before the citizens of Angel Heaven entirely forget the law," he finished.

"Right," I say slowly, "and how do I fit into this plan of yours? Because I'm still lost on that."

Ok, so I overdid the snark a bit on that one. It was still fun to watch my parent's expressions shift.

"We need you to study our law, find these holes and patch them up, since neither your mother, nor I have the time for it."

my father explained.

"You want me out of the way for something, don't you?"

I understand now, they're making some sort of preparation that I have to stay unaware of.

Neither of them denied it.

I'd had it for today; I stormed out and ran to my room, ignoring the multiple greetings I received from the lords and ladies I passed in a blur.

When I got back I noticed the maids had already been there my bed was made and fresh flowers were positioned by the window displayed in a vase.

'At least she remembers the ones I like.' I think.

This time they were the pink roses with the white flecks.

But the only scent that could have calmed me at that moment was the flower Dusk had created.

- Unbeknownst to Myra, Rick was the real creator of that flower. -

When I looked out I saw the sun was just about to set.

'Perfect timing.' I think.

Flying along the top of the arched corridors, I set about finding my older brother, Fidel.

We always went flying together when I was younger and my wings really needed a stretch.

I basically flew right into him just as I rounded the corner to the indoor gym.

My parents seriously hate the outdoors.

"Sorry." I blurt as I jump up.

"It's fine." He smiles as he gets up too.

"Remember, I can get you out but you have to stay in view of the Guards at all times or they might just fly after you again." He chuckles.

I love my brother, he's so easy going I find it hard to hold a grudge for even an hour before he gets me laughing and smiling again.

He looks really similar to me; same hair colour, though his is straight, exact same eye colour, pale features, well built frame, he has more strength and muscle than me though.

He's taller than me and three years older.

"Shall we go?" he asks just as we round a corner and I find myself face to face with my captors.

My eyes flash and I step behind my brother. He notices my tense state immediately and sees the guards eyeing us suspiciously.

"Good evening lads, I'm off for a quick flight around with my little sis." And we're outside again.

I really missed the wind in my hair, the smells of the city and the rising air currents beneath my wings.

Before Fidel even has a chance to sigh I'm off looping and twirling in the air, working the stiffness out of my wings.

He catches on quickly and tries to catch me since he always started off being it when we played tag as kids.

I'd learned a few new tricks though and he wasn't as agile and flexible as me. When he almost got me I'd rise or dive out of his way only to reappear behind him.

His expression told me he was enjoying it just as much as me, and still I could sense he was withholding something from me, something important.

So I give him a quick break from our flying tour before asking him, "What's bugging you? You seem a little distant."

"Don't worry about it." He dodges my question neatly.

I counter with a backhanded question of my own.

"So what happened between you and Sophia?" I say, already seeing him tense up.

"Look," he says tiredly, "I broke up with her, there's nothing more to it."

But suddenly his eyes burned and he looks at me. He was starting to scare me, I'd never seen him like that before.

"Please tell me you didn't." he said, disbelievingly.

"I did, and I miss him more and more everyday." I sigh sadly. His expression turns sympathetic, almost longing. "Fine, I'll tell you, but you have to promise not to say anything and not to freak out, okay?" he says.

"I promise." I say almost gleefully but I manage to turn it to curious.

He takes a deep breath. This is what my own parents wouldn't tell me, and he knows it.

"Father has arranged a marriage for you." He said it slowly, bluntly even. It still didn't take away the impact it had on me.

"Marriage?! Are you freak'in serious!" I say, careful to keep my voice moderate.

He can still sense my emotion though, especially with his gift of the 'Hearts Eye' and he chooses to leave it at that for the day.

"It's getting cold out, we'd best head inside."

I knew that was all I was getting out of him for today, and he knew I wasn't going to let the subject drop until I knew everything.

'Especially the Who.' I think determinedly.

Just as I step into the foyer it starts to snow.

I wasn't going to get that information out of him anytime soon though since I was stuck, no, locked in my room until I finished that stupid law study. Still I had something to mull over and it was no small piece of information either.

What's more I had an important piece of information for myself that no-one in the palace knew which would come in handy should I need to haggle for more information.

When I reach my room the window is already frosted over and the flowers are already starting to wilt.

'Why do we take beauty that only lasts a short while when we could go to that beauty where it could live, as anything living deserved?' I ponder. 'It's as if we think plants are dead.'

The thought scared me and I quickly pushed it away and as I did a new presence entered my mind and sure enough Rick was looking for me.

'Myra? Myra where are you? Myra!'

I finally figured out why he couldn't sense me, I was blocking him off, oops.

'Rick? Rick are you still there?'

I feel the pressure of his conscious intensify as we finally establish a working connection by the window.

'Myrelle! Are you alright? Where are you? Why couldn't I reach you before?'"

I laugh at his concern and soon so does he.

'You are okay though?' he asks more seriously this time.

'Of course I am. I wish you could meet my parents and my brother. He'd adore Rose, as a sister.' I say laughing again at the situation was just that unreal to me.

'We're coming for you.' he said.

'No! Not yet. Let things settle down a bit. It's chaotic right now and security is crazy. I can't even go for a joy flight without someone's company. I'll contact you again if there's a change of plans though.'

I reassure him.

'Guess what I found out?'

I tease him excitedly.

"From the way your emotions are going crazy I'd say it's a good piece of information or you wouldn't be so jittery," he replied lightly.

"Fidel broke up with Sophia!" I shriek happily.

'Then it's no wonder she was so uptight when she caught Rose. I knew there had to be some connection…'

Now he's musing, our connection fading.

'And one more thing.' I say, afraid that he'll leave me alone again, 'my father has seen fit to organize my wedding for me.'

Rick is immediately focused on me again.

'What? Why? When? Where? And for crying out loud with Who!?'

Now he's really annoyed.

'I don't know.'

I cry because I wish I knew these details as much as he does.

'I'll tell you when and hopefully we can figure out something to get me out of that situation without me having to make a run for it. But tradition demands I be given a week's notice before the wedding is to take place. So when I receive that I'll contact you.' I finish.

'Alright but I wont wait any longer than a week until next I hear from you otherwise I'll expect the worst and come for you,

and to answer your first question, we're all safe. Rose, Melody and Storm are fine and once Melody finds out your home she'll go back to you. She's already bursting with questions as it is, so expect her arrival soon.'

Now I'm the one letting the connection slip.

'And Myrelle? Love you. Sleep well.'

He doesn't wait for a reply, he just severs the connection. "Love you too." I whisper into the night just as two goldfinches come to rest on my windowsill, warming themselves by the light from my room. I open the window startling them but they fly inside out of the cold anyway, resting on a chosen perch at the head of the bed, and suddenly I notice how tired I am.

As I crawl into bed I almost miss the two voices of the Goldfinch's trill.

'Sleep Myrelle, we will keep watch for you, we will protect you, we will stand by your side for as long as our lord and lady ask.'

What I did know was that the mark of the Goldfinch was the Royal symbol for the Golden Kingdom, and that Rick was the Prince of that kingdom was also within my knowledge.

That night a set of brown and green eyes watched me sleep while a pair of Blue eyes looked out for Melody as she sped towards the palace.

I'm woken up by the whinny of an Alacorn tapping her snout against my window.

"Melody!" I cry happily.

I quickly change into an appropriate attire to ride her and rush outside. A trail of Guards follow me, alarmed by my speed, and oblivious to my yet unknown destination.

My boots crunch the hardening snow underfoot and Melody comes down from my window in a flash to greet me. The problem was that she's been gone from the palace for three years and had been almost half her size when last the guards had seen her so the form a circle around me pointing their spears at her.

"What are you doing?" I cry, outraged.

"Don't you recognize Melody?" I ask.

The commotion had drawn many a person to the palace's front garden including Fidel, and my parents, all of whom recognized Melody immediately.

After all, Fidel was the one who had trained Melody in the areas I didn't yet understand or was too small to help,

which was why Melody sprang on him nuzzling his neck lovingly.

The guards resumed their assigned positions, clearly ashamed of their misinterpretation.

"You reacted quickly and efficiently, you would have saved my life were Melody a threat to my wellbeing." I call after them.

Praise was rarely given out from my family though all I had done was state the truth.

Fidel was dazed from the impact of Melody's jump but was managing okay.

"Good to see you again too." He laughed as she gave him another playful nudge.

When Rick had said 'soon' I'd though it'd take her at least a couple of days to reach me, but her magic had gotten stronger and she herself had gotten stronger too.

'Now tell me, is there somewhere near Myrelle where I can stay, or must I reside in the stables this time?' She directed her question at my father but it was my mother who answered her.

"The Stables are right below Myrelle's room, however, should it be too cold for you we could arrange a guest room to better accommodate you."

'The cold does not bite nor sting me as it does your sensitive skin. I would be more than happy to stay there, with proper food and water servings, of course.' It was phrased as a question but was more of a statement than anything else.

"Of course," my mother complied.

"You are more than welcome to enter the palace if it be your wish." my father added almost hastily.

After all, Melody was the daughter of the two most powerful angel animals in all history. It would be good to have her as an ally, which they already did through me.

"Come, I'll show you where I stay." I say, letting the crowd part for me instead of pushing through them.

In the safety of my room I collapse and Melody relaxes.

'I'd forgotten the price Royal etiquette demands when used for long conversations.' Melody chuckled through our mental link.

'I told you it was a good idea to practice that type of etiquette, but you wouldn't listen, would you?' she continues before noticing the two Goldfinches.

'My highest regard of apology my lord and lady. I was so caught up in my discussion, I completely missed you.

It's good to see you again Amber and Jasmine.'

Melody had included me in her metal link with the two goldfinches, and from the intimate tone and the mention of their names I guessed she knew them fairly well.

'It's an honour to meet with you again on such friendly terms, Melody Alacorn.' trilled Jasmine, the one with the green eyes.

'Were you sent?'

Melody asks, curious.

'Yes, though they both know not that they called and asked us to.' Melody sighs.

'We'll have to show them the extent of their powers before they kill themselves, even if by accident.' Melody says.

'Aqua and Cristal are well, Aqua's Lady learned and uses her powers very wisely. She was looking out for you only a moment before.'

Amber inserted.

'I'm glad to know she's indeed still alive after that night.'

Melody says.

'Would you excuse us? As we must depart.'

Melody asks politely.

'Do as you wish Melody Alacorn.'

They indicate their leave and Melody drags me to the door.

With the connection severed with the goldfinches she says to me.

'You were right, Misty is alive!'

After I hear that, all I can think is,

'What?'

Only later do I realize the true implications of what I'd just found out.

CHAPTER 26: RICK - STAGGERING SURPRISES

Relief coursed through me at the knowledge Myrelle was safe, but what the hell was her father thinking arranging her marriage for her!

My worry and obvious jealously spoke for itself.

Melody had left as soon as she knew where Myrelle was, leaving me to wrestle with my thoughts alone.

I knew I had to get her out of there but Myrelle was right about one thing.

We needed patience and the Law on our side if we wanted to solve this little dilemma as peacefully as possible.

Still I wasn't good at doing nothing, and then there was, of course, the problem with Rose.

She hasn't stopped nagging me about her crown.

She still doesn't know it's hers.

The right words were just never there.

I couldn't tell her she was the Princess of a Fallen Kingdom without arousing hundreds of questions from her, to which

I didn't even know the answers myself...

Still, if I didn't tell her soon we'd both have some major problems.

So for the hundredth time I tried again and this time I actually found the right words.

"Hey Rose." I called her over and she came bouncing up to me, her crown gleaming on her head.

"Look... do you know whose crown that is you're wearing?"

Her response was obviously impatient; she rolled her eyes and shook her head. "Well... It's yours. You're one of the Princesses of the Golden Kingdom."

Now she interrupted me. "You mean the one now known as the Fallen Kingdom?" she piped up.

"Yes."

A simple answer which for once made her think instead of talk.

You know the saying third time lucky? Well, talk about hundredth time lucky!

"So the eye of the bird matches the eye of the owner?" she asked and I sighed; I knew she'd have some questions.

"Yes. Your green eyes are reflected in the bird's eye, just like my brown eyes are reflected in the bird's eye on my crown," I explain.

"When I placed the crown on my head my eyes almost glazed over. It seemed like I could hear every animal all around me

and they were all saying different things, is that normal?"

I knew exactly what she meant.

"Yes, it happened to me too. Your eyes glaze over and reflect your eye colour; it seems to be connected to your strongest angel power. I felt the rush of the wind, the pull of the ocean, the song of the forest, the warmth of the fire and the strength of the Earth course through me, talking and listening to me. It's an eerie but wonderful feeling." I try to describe it to her as best I can remember.

Why did you just say all those things when you only got that fire healing power?" Rose asks slowly.

Damn.

Another piece of information I was hoping to obscure from her. She's become very observant over the last few weeks.

Ever since Myrelle joined us, I realize.

Another positive effect she had on us.

God I miss her. I remember how I just cut her off after I told her I loved her. In truth I was just too scared to hear her reply; even I can feel afraid.

Now I'm wondering what her response would have been. Unfortunately Rose wont allow for me to daydream very long.

Apparently her curiosity is still unsatisfied.

"Well?" she asks impatiently.

"Melody gave me a gift of her own." I start wearily.

"She called it a natural gift, and I made the distinction of what was natural. That's what makes it seem like I have so many powers," I state indifferently.

"So that's how you opened up those water-wind cages..." she speculated.

"Yeah, and just so you know. The bird on your Crown is a Goldfinch with spread wings." I add.

"Did it really have gold wings? Are they really extinct?"

she asked, already looking awed.

"No, just the tips of their wings were Gold and that's only for those who were bound to us through our crowns, and yes, they are extinct as far as Angel Knowledge goes." I add again, giving her more information than I originally intended.

"Really!"

Now I have her attention again.

"What are their names?" she asks, and I'm really nearing the end of my patience with her.

"What do you think?" I manage a gentler tone.

"Green..." she murmurs, falling into the depths of her thoughts.

'Finally...' I think.

'Don't drift off now; it's about get interesting.'

A voice whispers in my head, and so I stay alert.

'Who are you?' I ask, directing my train of thought through my natural power.

'You'll find out soon enough.' The voice was high with an amazing song range.

'Almost birdlike', I think, certainly.

"Jasmine." Rose murmured so quietly I almost missed the name.

As soon as the name left her lips, Jasmine appeared before her, her golden wingtips winking in the midmorning sunlight. "You called and I have come." she crooned fondly.

"Myrelle and Melody are well, but why did you call me?" Jasmine pondered aloud.

Rose was still stunned at Jasmine's appearance.

"Well…" she stammered.

"Would you be so kind as to continue looking out for Melody and Myrelle?" she asked quietly.

"You needn't fear upsetting me." Jasmine laughed.

"Just tell me what you want me to do and, if I can, I will," she stated simply.

And that's exactly what she did.

"Please look out for Melody and Myrelle," Rose commanded, though still kindly.

Just before she left, Jasmine threw a glance my way and called, "Should you need your helper, simply call her as your sister did."

And then she was gone, the wind whispering tales of her flight, the legendary, 'and supposedly extinct,' I add in my head. Goldfinch.

'Could it have been her who spoke to me?' I ask myself, already knowing the answer.

Her voice had been too high and carried less music and strength than the other one had.

What would my Goldfinch's name be..?

And soon I'm pondering all sorts of names.

Auburn, Brunetta, Sorrel, Sable, Shade, Flame, Ofir, Pazel, Blair, Sandy, Trichia, Siena, Cinnamon.

None of them fit.

It became obvious pretty quickly.

Still I felt compelled to keep trying until I figured it out.

'At least it's something to do.' I think, as my thoughts turn bitter.

Who would be wealthy enough to convince a King of such high status to allow him his daughter's hand in marriage! Whoever it was, he had a smooth tongue and was VERY lucky.

Still, if tradition was anything to go by, we had about a month before the wedding day was announced.

'What am I supposed to do for an entire month?' I ask myself, agitated.

Rose has gone off into the woods exploring her surroundings and for once I don't follow her, I just let her be. She had to learn sometime.

Just as that thought disappeared, I was plunged into darkness.

At first there was nothing but inky blackness, then, it became a small pinprick distant and indistinct. Then it grew, becoming clearer, nearer and all I could do was gape as my older sister walked towards me. Her skin glowed and her halo was atop her head. At first I was just speechless, then the questions began to form, the answers I so desperately wanted but was afraid of.

"Don't look so startled, who else would have pulled you into a vision?"

She giggled softly, and that's when I finally cracked.

"Where the hell have you been?! Why are you here now of all times?! And for crying out loud, how did you ever achieve your halo?!"

My voice edges on desperation but I've never been the pleading type so I force a scornful look, daring her to try and answer me, and surprisingly, she does.

"Whoa. Slow down Rick. You're making me dizzy just listening to you." She smiles sheepishly before continuing. She holds up her index finger saying,

"First off, I've been trying to reach you when Myrelle isn't around."

I scowled, trying to hide my blush, then scoffed. "Why on earth would you need to get me alone after I'd met Myra?"

I say the name with a finality that surprises even me and Silvia's gaze grows sad.

"For the very reason you miss her." she explains gently before I even have time to figure out what she means. Then her middle finger joins the index in the air.

"Secondly, I'm here to give you some useful information to pass the time," she pauses, adding quietly, "and to warn you."

Again she continues before I can grasp her meaning, holding her thumb up as well.

"Finally, I achieved this." She pointed at her glowing white halo.

"By sacrificing myself for someone I cared about. In doing so I've become trapped in this place, where some of you angels see your visions of the future and of the past." she finished.

"So then that really did happen." I muse before I can stop myself and we both know what I'm talking about.

I can still see every detail, every facet of that image where Silvia fell from the balcony, blood trailing her body. Reaching, but not far enough.

"That's what I meant. I saved Misty, and in doing so managed to save both her and me from certain death."

And that's when she disappeared, but with no fault of her own,. It was me who was being pulled into that same horrific scene but this time I saw through Silvia's eyes instead of my own.

Cold stone pressed against my back, Misty clinging to my skirt as if I could lend her my strength. If only I could!

Those predators will find us soon, we have to get out of here, but that would alert the rest of them to take action.

"I can't be responsible for the fall of my own kingdom!"

I'm so torn and conflicted that I don't notice them straight away.

They scurry up the walls like rats, clinging to the sides with their sharpened talons and shining claws.

The others are safe. I can take comfort in that.

Now we're really boxed in.

They're everywhere and before I can even react one of them snatches Misty from my side. She was so scared that some of the fabric of my dress ripped in her hands.

Another masterpiece ruined. Ophir would kill me if these guys don't first, that at least cheers me up.

They're holding her at arm's length; she's crying and screaming as they lift her off of the floor by her hair.

Fury takes the place of wistful thoughts but as I see them all lined up proudly, I know they've been forced into this; they weren't to blame for this.

The real problem was the guarded secret kept hidden in the alcoves of The Institution.

We're all innocents forced into this fray by our superiors. This problem has to be ripped out at the roots, if we could only find the courage and time to keep digging.

This needs to end!

With that I make a lunge for the Griffin holding Misty. His surprise is so great that he even loses his balance a bit, giving me the opportunity to make a dive for him (and Misty).

I catch Misty around the waist and throw her in the direction of the balcony, giving her enough time, altitude and a head start to fly into our forest, hopefully making it across the border to Angel Haven.

I'd managed to save my sister, but I myself was at a loss.

My wings were tucked into my cardigan and the other predators had been roused by my sudden display of ferocity. I was pushed to the ground, claws dug into my back and I could feel my muscles snapping as twelve sets of sharp talons and gleaming claws ripped into my right side.

I pretend to faint and they roll me off the balcony. I drop like a feather, curiously enough, drifting and darting around.

I can see my own blood trailing after me, trying to catch up to my body. As I near the ground I close my eyes and accept defeat. My thoughts going out to my younger siblings, I feel a tingling sensation start near my shoulder blades at the base of my wings and spread through to my wing tips.

A pounding beat begins to tap in my head, my heart's song repeated over and over.

A blinding flash of light emanated off of me, causing everything around me to bend with the wind and glow from the light, and with the final note resonating in my head I feel my halo above me, before I really faint and the earth swallows me up.

I fall into a soft, warm autumn light.

I snap back to Silvia half aware of the present and half aware of her.

"Did you do that?"

I was breathing heavily, afraid to see the gashes inflicted on Silvia's body that I'd just relived.

Her mouth tips up into that humoured half smile of hers.

'If I could do that then I might actually be able to rip out and burn those roots myself.

As it turns out, it seems you've been graced with that task.'

Her expression turns bitter as she fades away. I snap out of my trance, gasping for air. Out of the corner of my eye I see Sarah looking at me intently, when she notices my gaze she shows her fangs in a dangerous smile that makes me shudder. Hold on…

If she's here where are Sebi and Crisanta?

As if on cue the two cubs roll out of the woods entangled playfully with each other.

"Do you know where Rose is?" I almost plead but pardon myself enough to show some restraint.

Again I'm signalled with that dangerous fanged smile.

'You're so special and yet you still worry about minute details, never bothering to even try to decipher yourself.'

I froze, did a retake and collapsed onto a seat like boulder. "Since when can I understand you guys?" I ask, not bothering to hide my exasperation.

'You should know the answer to that Rick.' Sarah said, her fur rippling with pleasure at my confusion, when it finally dawned on me.

"Of course," I murmur aloud.

"My natural ability includes all natural ornaments, inanimate or not, meaning I can basically understand everything, since everything that's ever been made has some natural quality in it.

That's when the sound started. First it was a soft humming, then it turned to a low buzzing getting louder and louder as I understood the full implications of Melody's gift.

That humming and buzzing was every conversation going on within my hearing range the conductors being every natural living and inanimate creature around.

When I slammed up my mental barriers I was able to keep their voices out.

'Very good, you've made further progress then I first thought.'

Sarah purred loudly.

'Furthermore, Melody isn't the only one who can create and bandy about gifts. Your sisters have already received one each from me.' she declared, daring anyone or anything to deny her passage of script. Not one creature raised its voice against her.

"You're well respected." I note.

"Which sisters do you mean though? I have three." I say and her fur hackles in response before she grows thoughtful. "Actually, in a manner of speaking, it's four, but that's beside the point. I've given your sister, Misty the power to see one's Aura. Your sister Rose, is still to receive her gift from me, though I will attend to that momentarily, and your sister Silvia received the gift of Wanderer. She's able to appear to anyone in an unconscious state or in an otherwise occupied mind,

"So she really is alive..?"

I wasn't expecting to feel happy for the rest of the week but that sentence was more than enough to renew my spirit and hope.

"Wait.." I falter, "Did you just mention something about another family member?"

It took all my self-control not to throttle the poor animal then and there.

Again, she just tipped the corner of her mouth up in that sad half smile of hers and melted into the forest's undergrowth before I can think to pursue her.

I slump against the Rock, half closing my eyes and enjoying the filtering sunlight, the soft bird song rippling through the trees and the occasional bursts of playful growls emanating from the two cubs.

In that very moment when I was about to fall asleep,

a different song flowed through the elements.

Its song was sad, full of sorrow and longing.

Its melody was in a minor key, vibrating off every surface, surrounding me. Strangest of all was the fact that I recognized the tune. It had been played at a funeral I'd attended when I was still very young. My memory suddenly gave me a flash and a name slipped from my mind to my lips as I spoke quietly,

"Reiko."

The twin who'd been caught and died in the fires of the Fallen Kingdom, while I'd managed to escape, all those years ago.

A tear falls free, rolling down my cheek as I struggle to recall what she'd looked like, but I could manage no more than a fuzzy outline of a face and wavy brown hair.

Unbeknownst to me, that funeral song had been sung by a bird that was supposedly extinct...

CHAPTER 27: MYRELLE - A DEADLY SECRET, A DYING LINEAGE

Happy days rolled by, yet as the clouds drifted back, the sun dispersed behind a wall of darkening clouds.

I was called to the castle's dining area to attend, as my maids kept saying, a very important dinner.

Considering that it was a dinner invitation I decided to dress well.

I picked out a low backed light blue ball gown laced with silver thread and slip it on over my head.

I opt for my silver tiara and then turn my attention to my make-up and jewellery.

A shock awaits me when my gaze falls on my reflection. I'd noticed my strength fading over the past few days and had forgotten all about Rick, but being out of contact for so long meant I was left weak and vulnerable.

I had to talk to him again, had to see him again, just once.

I knew we would energize each other so why was he ignoring me?

I couldn't fool myself though…

I knew why he was doing it, but it was costing us both dearly. 'Soon,' I think, 'soon I will see him again.'

The thought gave me hope and I clung to it as I readied myself for the upcoming dinner with my parents.

I decide to go for Blue Topaz incorporation today wearing my hair down in free curls and weaving strands of blue topaz and delicate silver chain into some of them.

Next, I add my blue topaz earrings to the ensemble, then I clasp my silver blue necklace on and I'm about to add a plain silver ring embedded with diamonds when my window bursts open.

I can see and hear the wind howling outside but not a breeze stirs in my room.

Realization sinks in when Stardusk floats into the room on a cushion of gathered air.

Her petals are fading and she doesn't even have to ask before I rise from my sitting position and go about finding her a bowl of water.

'Thank you.' Her conscious brushes mine in simple relish.

'A gift for you from Rick.' the flower says and lets her petals rustle open.

I was honestly at a loss for words when I beheld his gift, it was a ring, and brilliantly crafted too.

A sea blue sapphire sat at its centre and ringed by diamonds. When the ring I held in my hand came into contact with the ring resting in Stardusk's pollen the two merged creating a ring of simple perfection.

The ring had a silver band that looked like a leafy vine, and while the sapphire was unchanged the diamonds had acquired some of the blue topaz's colour, now looking like the sky covered with a thin misty veil; the diamonds had the faintest tinge of blue to them now. In short, it was the perfect gift for the girl of your dreams.

'Where did he get this material? This ring?' I ask, still admiring the ring.

Amusement emanated from the flower.

'He made it from his Dream and Nature Power. The only non-magical thing on this ring is the sapphire that he found in an abandoned gem mine just yesterday.'

Now my attention snapped up.

'You mean he somehow made his powers merge, turned his powers physical and incorporated his emotions into this design!?'

It was so outlandish and had never been done before. I started to worry about him.

'Is he okay? He shouldn't have wasted his powers on this for me.'

This gains the flowers full attention.

"You know how to do that too."

One of her petals gestured at the ring in my hand.

'And he's fine, only those who are bonded opposites have the strength, courage and power to make these creations but that describes the two of you perfectly.'

The flower was about to leave when she seemed to remember something.

'By the way, he also incorporated some magical protection charm into the ring as well. I'll be seeing you again Princess, farewell for now.'

Stardusk's conscious faded as she drifted away, leaving me with a gift I honestly didn't think I deserved but I placed it on my finger anyway, wanting to have something physical to remind me of him.

I'm supposed to meet my parents in an hour and I'm really getting bored. I change into casual attire again and lay my outfit on my bed for when I need it.

I decide to check in on Fidel and find him at his usual hangout by the Gym.

I can see that look on his face that suggests he's deep in thought.

"Hey Fidel." I call out to him, causing him to jump in surprise.

"Hi." He sounded uneasy, and that's unusual.

"What are you doing out here?

Isn't there supposed to be some important dinner happening soon?"

Ok... Very unusual, what's wrong with him?

I sigh, "I'm so bored and dinner isn't until eight."

I gesture to the watch that reads five past seven. He nods in understanding.

"I need to get some air," I say, "think you could come out with me for a while?"

He takes the bait without me even having to jiggle the string.

"Sure."

He answers simply, he's definitely uneasy.

With that I'm spirited out of the palace and into the warm night air.

A breeze ruffles his hair but he's too preoccupied to notice. "You okay?" I ask him quietly.

He responds with a sigh. Talk about turning tables.

"Not really. Sophia's been on my back ever since she finished that mission."

That got a flare of anger out of me.

"She keeps talking about some Angel Hunter who she's going to track down when released from her duty."

Now he was starting to scare me.

'What a cliché.' I think dryly.

"When's she going to be released from duty?" I ask, relieved to have a subject of interest.

"After your wedding." came the blunt reply.

"Why so bitter?" I ask playfully.

"You'll find out momentarily." he answered sadly then he walked away leaving me standing there, the evening breeze washing over me, blowing my hair to the side and pulling at my clothes, its song guided me and I decided to follow.

I found myself by the little pond where Fidel and I had played as kids.

I couldn't handle it.

I broke down, sobs escaping my throat and tears marring my make-up.

Standing over a long lost memory, I looked up to see a glint of gold, my senses sharpened.

Isn't moonlight ghostly silver or white?

This day was really too much, I was unnerved and late!

I ran to my room and re-applied my make-up in record time before dashing to the main dining hall.

My arrival was announced and I stepped into the candlelight-dining hall.

"Sir, Ma'am." I curtsy to each of them in turn.

They nod their approval and I take a seat.

"What's this all about?" I ask tentatively.

My mother smiles sadly, but it is my father who speaks. "This." He gestures grandly.

"It's about a long lost truth, a truth of great value, a truth of great importance and a truth of great sadness."

His entry complete, he launches into a story I'd never heard before.

"Three realms all live in harmony, each realm has a ruling kingdom and a ruler. Each realm is split into sectors governed by allocated Royals, like us.

One of each of these Kingdoms harbors a pair of strong spell weavers, known as opposites... or twins.

Each pair of opposites have the ability to forge a bond between them.

Should all opposites become bonded with each other and work together, they can open a passage to a place that holds the key to control in all our three realms, and should just one ordinary being seek this key they will be stopped at all costs, by the guardians of the key's location and by the opposites of the three realms.

Should the opposites and the guardians clash against each other, than this era of peace and prosperity will end and the guardians will die, whereas the opposites will be forced into the service of the key's holder.

But, if both the guardians and the opposites fight together, a new era would begin where conflict and negativity could no longer exist and only the purest of souls and kindest of hearts would be accepted into this place of new love and life."

He ends his story and I barely hear my mother's weeping. "Tell me, daughter, which sounds best to you?" he asks menacingly.

I gulp.

"The era we have now." I say automatically.

"But, we have to fight against this growing conflict, we must find a way to make peace with our enemies before this current conflict escalates to far worse conditions." I add.

My father smiles and my mother looks shocked at what I've just suggested.

"And how do you suppose we appeal to them?" my father whispers, a glint in his eyes.

"We must find a way of communication. We have to better understand them and maybe pull up barriers and land marks that Humans, Angels and Mer-people can comply with."

I purposely didn't mention the beings from the Demons Lair, but father hadn't seen a need to mention them either so I didn't see a problem there. This clearly wasn't what my father had wanted me to say, but my mother's expression showed that I'd made the right choice and said the right thing.

"Very well, what kind of barriers were you thinking of?" Though still displeased with my former answer, I could see a new plan coming together in my father's mind.

My spirits plummeted.

"I'd have to see what humans best respond to and find similarities between our two races, if we need defences right away I'd suggest encircling each Kingdom or area with a physical barrier that has only four entries. The northern, southern, eastern and western gates, that shall be locked and guarded at all times and only those who we wish to enter or exit will then be allowed to do so."

I snatched up the first idea I'd managed to find, which was very similar to what the Golden Kingdom did in the olden days of conflict, war and hatred.

Again my words left my father raking his head for a new plan.

My mother had other ideas though.

"Darling. We agreed to discuss this at a later time, privately. We have more important and pressing matters to attend to first."

She gave him a chilling look, which he answered with a piercing gaze of his own.

"Very well."

He sounds exasperated now.

"Your wedding is taking place in a week."

That left me groping for self-control and proper composure,

I was that shocked.

When I found my tongue again I whispered,

"Why? Why did you do this?"

My eyes were tearing up but I wasn't backing down now.

My mothers' look turned sympathetic but my father wasn't caving.

"What reason or even right, do you have to control my love life, or, my life in general, for that matter?"

I ask, more dignified this time.

"To keep you safe," came the blunt reply.

"That's it! You're not going to elaborate on that? What does that even mean!?" I ask.

"It means, you have to keep your lineage safe, alive and most importantly you have to stay faithful to your line."

Ok, I got that, but what the hell did he mean by faithfulness to my line?

My expression was read pretty clearly.

"So you still don't know."

My father mused. Now my mother intercepted him again.

"We were the Golden Kingdom's biggest threat and opponent in the times of war. So we made a pact with them, we wouldn't interfere with each other in any way what so ever.

Meaning at age eighteen we married you to a suitable young man who had nothing to do with the Golden Kingdom, and the same was done for us in reverse."

When she paused for breath my father picked up her unfinished line.

"Both our lineages are close to extinction so it's important that we keep them both alive at all costs," he finished.

"Even at the cost of one's happiness and love?"

I whisper, tears escaping their prison.

My father nods solemnly and I practically run to the door where I pause momentarily calling back,

"Might I ask who my suitor is to be?"
Determination resonates in my voice.
"The Prince Aqua, of the Sea and Sky." my father answered.
I run to my room crying; I slam the door and sink to the floor.
Defeated.
Broken.
Lost.

CHAPTER 28: RICK - SLASHED WEDDING PLANS

How is it possible for such stupid coincidences to occur? Ever since she told me when, where and why, I was worried, but with the who unveiled I'm just sick of running into this guy. He's tried to capture us, he's out for world domination

and he's going to marry Myrelle in a week!

I can't imagine living without her and yet that's just what I'm doing.

I need to see her again; it's relieving to talk to her through our mental link, but it's not the same as seeing her face to face.

Once I come to that conclusion I hear a whisper in the wind and a simple name jumps to the forefront of my mind. Slowly, realization sinks in.

'Amber...' And sure enough the glint of gold catches my eye and Amber hovers above me, wingtips glinting splendidly in the evening sun.

"Finally."

She sighs happily, song flowing from her open beak as her emotions peak with pride.

"I'm glad to know you've remembered me."

She sang and memories flooded back, me sitting in the recipient foyer waiting to see my parents.

Me listening patiently as my parents explain the new duties I'll have to take on board.

Me receiving a half oval shape with a cloth draped over it,

I pulled the cover off and four small gold finches met my eyes unflinchingly, each had a different eye colour; two brown, one green and one blue.

I looked at each in turn but when my gaze fell on the one with the darker brown eyes my own eyes glazed over and reflected an amber brown all around the room.

My parents gazed at each other with small triumphant smiles playing over their lips and that whispering name played over and over in my head like a rustling autumn breeze singing through the high treetops.

Amber, Amber, Amber...

I snap back to the present with a sharp whistling noise emanating from Amber herself.

"I thought you might need that."

Confused, I look at my lap and find a wedding invitation. Annoyed, I don't bother to look at the names before carefully refolding it and slipping it into my pocket.

I take to the sky with Amber tailing me.

'They've increased security around the area to try and avoid any inconveniences.'

Amber switches to thought sharing as the wind increases it's almost snapping song. She banters on and on and I listened to everything, absorbing every detail about the place.

'How do I get in?' I ask and a humourless chirp makes me reconsider reading that envelope.

'Who does this invitation belong to?'

That got Amber thinking for a while and still we neared our goal with a vigorously increasing pace.

A few hours later I land in a nearby tree canopy.

Confused thoughts assail me from Amber.

"Do you really expect me to wear this to a wedding?" I ask, gesturing to my worn clothes. "Besides, you need to rest and so do I."

With that we both fall asleep with the rising moon at our backs, thankful for the company we now shared and the rest we were now catching up on.

'Rick? You there?'

'Myra!' What was she doing, contacting me so late?

'What's wrong?' I answer diplomatically.

'What do you think Rick?' she snaps back, exasperated.

'I'm getting married in less than a week, I'm imprisoned in my own home, and, the Prince of the sea and sky is arriving tomorrow! By the way did you know his name was actually Danube? It means, Into the Black Sea. Not a bad idea in my position...' she murmurs and I was clearly not supposed to have heard it, but I did.

'Why can't you marry later in your life, once you've found the guy you love? It's madness to force you to marry someone you don't love.'

I try to understand what her parents are thinking.

'Because I have to keep my lineage alive, it's dying out and apparently yours and my kingdoms had a bit of a quarrel in the past decade... Besides it's not a high price I have to pay.'

Now she's trying to comfort me, she's very sweet but can really be pathetic at times.

'The price they're asking is the happiness and love of their princess! How is that not a high price!?' I shoot back.

'I don't like it either!' she screams, losing her composure too.

'What other choice do I have anyway?'

And before I can reply she says something that makes my

heart stop. 'I have found and felt love and it's the nicest feeling in the world but the happiness and love of my people is far more important than that of one selfish Princess.'

Now she's getting me mad.

'Myra! You are anything but selfish! You're a pure angel who always thinks of others over yourself.' I try to reassure her, I'm out of luck though.

'Thank you, I'll always remember you. Goodbye.' she whispers and I could have sworn a tear rolled down her cheek when she said that.

'I love you.'

It's a quick and fleeting thought, but I just had enough of a connection left to catch it.

"I love you too." I whisper into the night. The stars were the only ones to see a tear find freedom from my eyes and roll sadly down my cheek, only to drip off and sparkle briefly before disappearing into the black abyss below.

~

'He loves me too!'

I'd never felt so happy until I'd heard those words.

He didn't even realize he'd shared the thought with me, in fact,

if I know him at all I'd guess he's whispered it to himself.

I'd never know how close I'd come to the truth.

Though I slept peacefully that night, the next few days were chaotic with organization for the wedding taking place everywhere.

The bakers were arguing about the cake's size, type, icing and decorations.

"Excuse me? Could I help you with that?" I ask as they continue their banter back and forth. They freeze, only noticing my presence because I'd spoken.

"Your Highness..." they stammer in unison.

"What seems to be the problem?" I ask, smiling down at them.

"Well, we can't decide on the outer frills for the cake Princess Sapphire." one of them explains.

"Which two particularly?" I muse, scouting the numerous colours laid out on the table.

"Red or purple." They reply and one goes on to say, "Red is the colour of love so..."

Before he can continue another interrupts him, "Purple is the colour of Royalty though." he says, casting a glare in the direction of his co-worker.

"What about this one?" I ask, pausing before a lovely light blue, "and then add some of those white sugar crystals you have over the top of just the frills to catch the eyes of our guests?"

I contemplate the idea and bid them a polite farewell before carrying on with the Daily Wedding checks.

"Of course your highness." they murmur as I leave.

A few hours later I lay back on my bed, exhausted the light has already begun to fade when I remember something, and it's very important.

'The wedding dress!' I think despairingly and I recall my first encounter with Rick.

His foster parents were Joseph and Maria, the royal tailors of Angel Haven.

He'd been so composed and polite and our friendship had grown and endured for the past months where I'd been with him, so much so that I feel in love with him.

'Why..? Why did it have to be like this!?'

I'm crying now as I remember all the times he saved me, swooping in from above to catch me whenever I fell.

A forbidden love is a tragic love, unless something is altered...

An idea formed in my mind, a brilliant but dangerous idea. 'Love and Hate are separated by a single thread, if love is stronger it will turn hate to love.' I think, determined, and I fall asleep pondering my best tactical appeal.

~

A whole day spent shopping, you'd think I'd be thrilled but to be honest I'm completely lost on how girls can enjoy it so much. Still, I look presentable and Amber has brilliant taste when it comes to clothes.

Now I only have to pass the guards at the gate and make my way to Mother and Father, then the true test and the real fun can begin.

I know Myra like the back of my hand and what I'm going to try to pull off is going to take at least that much knowledge to work properly.

Mum would be so proud of me; she'll have to help me a bit. I'm no genius when it comes to sewing but I have great taste when it comes to matching colour to personality to an occasion.

I guess there's always a first time for everything, still I've never completely made a dress before, let alone a wedding dress.

'We'll just have to wait and see how it goes. After all, what could possibly go wrong with my parents to help me? Well, adoptive parents anyway...' I think sadly.

We'd travelled quite a bit yesterday and a day's flight away was Angel Haven.

With a start I remember the invitation in my pocket. Carefully, I pull it out and read through it. To be honest I was quite relieved when I read through it but it wasn't perfect either. It read:

Princess Myrelle Blue Sapphire
And
Prince Danube Hali Aqua
Request the honour of your Presence
Sir Pazel Arune
Treasure keeper of the former Golden Kingdom
At their wedding to be held on the 18th of May.

It was well set out and was decorated with the petals of a Blue Salvia flower but one petal looked somewhat out of place and as soon as I touched it I realized what it was.

Stardusk had let one of her petals blow into the invitation and I saw some of the silver dusting had smudged onto the paper and when I tried to rub it off I noticed a fainter writing below that of the polite wedding invitation.

Using the petal as a brush, I covered the invitation with the dusting and gasped as the hidden message was revealed, the handwriting was unmistakably Myra's, and it read;

"I hope this invite reaches you well. I'll be waiting for you in the front palace gardens the day before the wedding. Say nothing of this to anyone.
P.S. the dusting comes off with synthetic cloth, (if you have any)."

Now she was pushing me for time too. Well she deserves some respect, at least, and so I inscribed my replied message on Stardusk's petal and sent it blowing through the wind with my natural gift giving it direction and speed.
'It'll reach her soon enough', I think compliantly before refolding the invitation and placing it into my pocket again.
~
I'm still tired when I wake up during the night to the sound of a hushed conversation taking place in the room below mine. The stables, I realize and listen with strained ears as the conversation continues.
"…really necessary to take these precautions?" asks one person.
"The King's orders, though I'd pay my month's wage to know the reason." another replied.
"But why shouldn't the Princess find out?" the first speaker mused.
That brought me up short and I found myself lying on the freezing floor to better understand them.
"Who knows? But now that I think about it, isn't her room right above here?" the other realizes nervously.
A loud snort draws all three of us up short and I breath a quiet sigh of relief as Melody's voice breaks into my thoughts.
'I'm guessing you'll want an explanation for that right..?'
She sighed wearily.
'You read my mind.'
I send back.
This wrings an amused feeling out of her.
'I do that all the time, Myrelle, it comes with being your bonded angel animal. Meet me by the stables just before dawn, wear your riding gear and try not to be followed. I'll see you soon.'
I could just picture her tossing her mane to emphasize her point.
Casting a glance at the clock, I realize I have an entire hour to kill in my room before dawn will show her morning face.

So I'm about to check in with Rick when a trace of silver catches the moon's light, casting a shimmering sparkle in my direction.

I open the window and allow the petal to float in and I notice the slightest stir of magical energy in the wind.

'Rick.' I think, hopelessly letting a half smile play across my lips.

The moon's light catches the silver beautifully, sending delicate patterns cascading all around the room and as I look closer I see that the patterns are actually written runes conveying a very important message.

"Hey Myra, I'll meet you there, but, since when does Stardusk deliver messages? Anyways, see you then."

He can't be serious.

He is.

'Are you serious!?'

He didn't mention what the place was or when, he didn't even think to sign the stupid thing so that I could be sure it was him and not some weirdo who happened to be spying on me.

Talk about creepy.

Yikes…

Shit.

What is it with me and time lapse?

Now I've got five minutes to get changed and somehow sneak past the back guard.

I got changed in a snap and basically sprint down the silent hallway only to stop myself two doors down.

'Get a grip would you?' I scold myself.

After all, most of the palace guests are still asleep.

I move through the hallways as quietly as I can manage, gliding with lithe grace and before I know it I'm at the back gate and it's completely deserted. There isn't a soul in sight, guards included.

Though that fact is fairly worrying, I brush it aside since it's given me the exact opening I need to get out.

I'm glad I paused because just as I was about to creep out a blast of water magic strikes the very place I would've been standing had I not paused in thoughtful consideration of the oddities happening today.

I stop the instinctual shriek from rising to my throat since there are already plenty of maids doing that for me and it's unprincessly to shriek unless hurt.

In the confusion I slip past the magic weavers, using their created smoke screen as cover to get out of there.

I have a nagging suspicion that the attackers weren't just trying to hit me but I need all my focus to navigate this thickening mist. I see a flash of blended turquoise in the sky and fly up, right into a very anxious Melody.

I've ridden her bare backed many times so I easily settled onto the small of her back and grasped her mane for support before she speed off towards the Forest Spring.

'Thank god you're okay!' she breathes a whinny of relief.

'What was that about?' I ask, including her in my head. I don't want to admit it but I'm sort of scared.

'The Prince asked for your hand as a hoax. All he wants is the inheritance. When he found out that the inheritance of your kingdom didn't include him even in marriage he tried to take it forcefully, by using you as a hostage and a ransom.'

I knew it.

I hadn't said anything but even I have suspicions.

'What now then?' I ask quietly.

A twinkle sparked into existence in Melody's eyes.

I'd know that look anywhere.

'We rally up our little army.' both Melody and I think, simultaneously.

~

I woke up, startled out of sleep by a burning sensation in my pocket.

When I go to touch it, my fingers burn red hot.

Quickly reaching inside, I pull out a scorching hot wedding invitation.

'What the..?' I think and right before my eyes the Invitation disintegrates and a golden dust falls into my palm reading

'Cancelled' in swirling gold writing,

I let it blow away and think sardonically, 'What's she done now?'

Still, I'm surprised she managed to get it cancelled.

Normally they'd only delay or prolong events of such importance, and all I can think is: 'What have you done this time?'

I shake my head.

This was strange… even for Myra.

Yet I feel a smirk transform my features nonetheless.

CHAPTER 29: MYRELLE - SINCE WHEN?

Ordinary angels wouldn't be running for their lives through a forest.

Ordinary angels wouldn't have to build a wall of deception around them to keep their friends and family alive.

Ordinary angels wouldn't need to marry someone they didn't love to continue their family line, but hey, since when am I an ordinary angel anyway?

So, like I said before, I'm running for my life through a forest while being chased by the little Prince's Elite Guard just so that he can use me as a ransom to collect some of my heritage.

Apart from that I'm still worried about that vision and, oh yeah, that's right, I got my wedding cancelled which is going to anger my parents to no end. That is, unless I am actually captured—that'd be a whole different story.

The only positives I can contemplate right now are that Rick is safe and that Melody is with me.

Ok, so that's just the slightest bit selfish, but its not like I haven't tried to get her to leave, she just won't listen to me,

and, to be honest, I'm glad she's by my side.

I'm snapped back to the present with the sound of a loud snap.

"What was that?" I ask Melody. She's flying high above me and an idea hits me that I could be doing the same thing. Why does it always take forever for me to come up with these ideas!

I'm about to take off when I receive a warning signal from Melody:

"We've got air pursuers too. And that snap you heard was one of 'their' wings."

That brought me up short.

"You mean…"

I couldn't say it, but I remembered the pain of having to fight off a mental assault and actually felt sorry for the angel she'd overpowered.

Suddenly we burst into a clearing, not good.

Sure enough, they had us encircled in a matter of mere seconds.

Without any warning, Melody screamed a terrified whinny and a sinister laugh echoed around us. Clouds drifted in, blocking out the sun.

"That's right. Listen to your father." the voice purred and my blood turned cold as I recognized it.

'Marcus..?'

It was so absurd I almost dismissed the idea completely.

I was right though.

Marcus strolled out into the clearing followed faithfully by Melody's father, The King of the Unicorns.

"What the hell are you playing at!?" I ask, infuriated.

That gains me another of his chilling smiles.

"What do you think?"

I so hate guessing games.

"Why don't you just tell me?" I say through gritted teeth.

"Aww, you're such a spoil sport, but I'll go along with it…

for now." he answers dismissively.

"Now then, to put it bluntly, I want to control the world,

I'm using that stupid Prince as a distraction and soon I'll have that annoying tracker too."

This is going way too fast for me, but I do my best to absorb every word he says.

"Once I have all the opposites, or twins, as the case may be, I'll harness your power to defeat the guardians and take the key of control to rule over the entire world."

This is bad.

That's an understatement.

"Also, the marriage thing was just so I'd have some reserve cash and so I could lower your parent's guard. I'm surprised it actually worked."

Now he was musing.

"That link of yours should lure him in fast enough."

He grins suddenly and I find it has an even worse effect on me that his chilling smiles.

I grimace as he grips my upper arm, but I continue to keep Rick cut off from me.

That makes him outright laugh.

"You really think you have a chance of holding me off?" he was teasing.

I knew, but his words caught me off guard, for once.

I took every blow he slung at me while Melody did the same with her father.

~

Something's wrong.

She's purposely blocking me out and the more I try to ask her the harder she fights me off.

I need some clue, an image of a place, anything to tell me where she is.

I must be really worried because Amber noticed a frown flicker over my features and gave me a brilliant idea.

If she's somewhere natural, you should be able to sense her life force… maybe even her aura.

Slowly I lower my mental barriers and let my conscious seep into the earth, air and water spreading around the world and picking up the slightest vibrations.

Once I narrowed down my search area to Angel Haven I allow myself to slip out of my body into my aura to have a look around.

I'm astounded by what I see, every living thing has some kind of aura.

When I pass by the clearing I'd flown over earlier I pause, taking in a terrifying view.

I recognize Myra's aura immediately and there's something familiar about the other angel with her.

It was the other two beings in the clearing that worried me, one was Melody and the other, was a very powerful unicorn. They were in a full fledged battle against one another, their magical energy was expanding rapidly, their auras being consumed in the shining silvery-white glow of magic, possessing their minds and bodies.

'If that keeps up they'll kill themselves, and the after effects could be disastrous!'

I use my aura to beacon Myra, but as soon as her attention wavers she's consumed with pain and her attention focuses elsewhere.

'He's… trying to… lure you in.'

Myra was actually sparing some of her energy to warn me. She wasn't finished though, sending her most concerning emotions to me with a single name.

'Marcus.'

That was it, now she was fully focused on the physical battle taking place between her and him.

Marcus?

The name rang numerous warning bells in my head, and was still fresh in my memory.

But who was he?

Amber interrupted my musings with a sorrowful tune pulling me back into my body and away from the other auras and Myra.

'I'll help you.' I think surely.

~

He came!

He actually looked for me!

Those thoughts pushed me through the next few hours of physical fighting and assault.

I was seriously worried about Melody. Her eyes kept flashing darker and darker; she'd be lost in a magical void if this fight didn't end soon. Just then Marcus decided to change tactics, instead of attacking me directly he tried to pin me down.

We were both tired, our breathing heavy.

"If you won't break I'll just have to find your weakness."

When he lunged for me this time I took off instead of jumping out of the way, hoping to unbalance him, but luck had clearly deserted me in this instance. He'd been weaving a water web the entire time and I was too busy to even notice!

The ghost of a smile flickered over his features as I became entangled in his net.

~

I hid in a nearby tree.

None of them could see me, and still my heart ached for her when I saw Myra trapped in a water net; a sneer distorted her usually beautiful features.

What was worse was that Marcus was slowly edging around her. I'd seen the move done many times and the pain was excruciating should you be unlucky enough to get caught in a trap like that, but judging from his expression, Marcus was going to make her suffer as much as he possibly could.

Sure enough, with no warning whatsoever he sprung on her, took her wing in his hands and twisted it, spraining it badly.

Her scream must've echoed all the way to the palace since my ears were still ringing from that terrible sound.

After all she'd gone through she was still holding on, she didn't faint, nor did she back away. She just stared at him with cold eyes.

Melody's father stopped his assault momentarily, sharing the pain his daughter felt, then he shook his head and continued attacking her in any magical way possible.

'He only uses magic...' my lips quirk in understanding.

'The Unicorn King was forced to bond with Marcus because he was his former bonded angel's closest relative. The bond isn't genuine though.'

I think.

His physical strength must've diminished from countless battles won by only using magic.

They were still looking for Myrelle's weakness, but I'd found theirs.

Meanwhile, Melody was being led into a similar trap, the difference was that Melody was too smart to fall into a simple trap as such had been created. She evaded every trick used on her and teased her agitated assailants ceaselessly.

It was even beginning to bother Marcus, I saw, as he flinched slightly every time his companions failed to capture Melody. Countless, useless strategies came to mind all of which I dismissed.

The perfect opportunity came and I had no time to hesitate. Melody had tossed her mane wildly in an attempt to confuse her assailants and give her the opportunity to help Myra out of the water web.

She was quickly brought back under control, but, no one had thought to look up so I had the perfect opening.

I flew down on silent wings using the opportunity to block out the sun with some clouds. As soon as one of them noticed me I went into a dive and took him out before he even had the chance to utter a single word.

Now, I had their attention though.

~

He never stopped moving, a single wrong move by his opponents and they were wiped out. Each move was lethal and he never missed his target.

I could see Marcus losing his snark along with his confidence as he beheld the scene where all but two of his companions were scattered, unconscious around the clearing.

I'm surprised to see Marcus still holding his ground and even more so when he begins to leisurely stroll towards him. Warnings of all sorts flash through my head, none of which I even have time to analyse before another quickly replaces the earlier one.

'He's far too confident.' I think,

and the unconscious warning easily and quickly reaches Rick.

He never drops his guard, nor does he attempt any funny tricks or evasive motions. He goes towards Marcus at a full forced run, his shoulder ramming into Marcus's chest, the impact sending him flying back quite a ways and his surprise is evident. Obviously he'd thought something was going to happen that didn't.

But why didn't it happen?

My suspicious nature nagged at my conscious but I had to stay focused.

A tug at my conscious sets my thoughts on the air pursuers, and realization strikes like a lightning bolt on a stormy night. I send an approving sensation to Melody and receive an amused feeling tinged with defiant pride in reply.

With my focus wavering an idea seems to spark in Marcus's eye.

He makes a flip-like jump over Rick and lands right beside me. His breathing is ragged, his clothes unkempt and his eyes shining with a rare emotion for any angel... mad terror.

Here's the problem with a seriously scared angel: they'll go to any length to escape, including drastically measured actions.

I wasn't far off, he pulled out a dull knife that gleamed ghostly silver grey in the early moonlight.

That's when I notice something else, something far more sinister than the knife being pressed against my neck.

The magical energy was disappearing... and it was true,

the dark magical essence was slipping away.

'Since when was that part of a magical battle?' I think.

'Since Never.' comes the grim reply from Melody.

A spark of recognition suddenly ignites in my mind just as Rick opens our mental connection, and I feel a fast flash of a thousand words, a single image from one encounter, and we both shiver as we recognize the dangerous, and most probably insane, angel before us.

Marcus.

My body tenses at just the thought of his name.

He was one of the Angels who'd held us captive, and, he'd used the chain on me to try and control my movements.

A low hum vibrates in my ears, and I recognise the dangerous growl of predators rimming the shadows of the clearing.

Fear wasn't an emotion on my mind right then, but anxious described me pretty well, especially on behalf of an oblivious Rick and a distracted Melody.

While my expression had turned to one of unclear confusion as so many thoughts flurried through my mind,

Ricks could be read pretty clearly.

He was, quite simply put, mad as hell.

Heck, even that, was putting it lightly.

CHAPTER 30: RICK - DROPS OF BLUE BLOOD

Blood seeps from a severe wound on Melody's back.

It looks like a bite wound but that's even more confusing than the fact that her father seems to be…

In the split second it took for me to realize what I was about to think, I didn't get a chance to react when Marcus howled angrily, his face contorted into a mask of mottled rage and the fear in his eyes disintegrated as he realized for himself what had happened.

What had indeed happened was that Melody had bested her father at his own game, and he'd paid the price for his loss.

Still… that didn't explain the physical wounds Melody had obviously received from the fight.

~

Right on cue Melody walked toward Marcus slowly, each hoof leaving a print in the ground and when she reached him he holds his composure in an act of defiance even I wouldn't have attempted.

Even the sky has darkened and the moon vanishes behinds layers of wispy clouds that thicken before crying at the loss of a Royal.

The rain glows with moonlight, each drop infused with some of the moon's mourning spirit. Every drop that hits the ground is a cool colour, blue, green, purple and black, but further into the forest the raindrops hit the body of the unicorn King and begin to glow with his remaining energy shining brighter than the stars.

With the process complete, the Unicorn King's Spirit Aura is transferred to Marcus and he painfully relives his partner's death.

With the process complete, the clouds recede and the moon's eye watches us expectantly with the stars as her witnesses. We wait patiently to see what effect the transformation will have on him.

No sound, no warning, no hope.

Marcus's eyes snap open, his body now infused with the pure blue blood of his dead bonded-angel-animal, his aura encased in a temporary golden shine and silver glow. A warning is on my lips just as the clearing seems to shift and we're in the arena of my home. Dread clutches my heart as I realize what happened.

Tears blur my eyes and the only reliable thought I have is,

'The vision is happening now!'

The predicament I'd gotten myself into slapped me hard in the face and before the weeping sound had even left her throat I knew Misty was behind me, bruised, bloodied and badly injured. No doubt thanks to those stealthy predators, lurking near Marcus.

When the first sob escaped the girl's throat I was already way ahead of time.

I knew what was going to happen if I wasn't fast enough.

I knew where I had to go and I knew what I had to do, and boy, it wasn't going to be easy.

I tear across the sky like an arrow shot from a taut bowstring.

When I finally reach the arena I find it absolutely packed to its maximum capacity.

I'm beaconed over and ushered into the royal quarters for the rare matches we hold here.

Distorted Reality.

I'm awed and overshadowed by this rare display of magic ability, especially on this scale.

Even though I know what I will see, my stomach still lurches as I behold Rick and Marcus, armed only with their bodily abilities, strength and minds.

But I could tell something was wrong. Rick seemed to be dazed, and totally out of what was happening around him.

~

I saw all this through Myrelle's eyes before my attention was demanded elsewhere and it wasn't a second too late before I felt Marcus's fist barely miss my face.

'So that's what we look like when we see through the eyes of another...'

I can tell I'm frustrating him, he's beginning to get a little careless with his attacks now, and his footing falters rather than steadies his balance. He's tiring quickly, most of his energy expanded when he created this illusion, and I'll credit him on his attention to detail 'cause not a single facet of this place is missing or wrong.

Still, he'd worked up the nerve to challenge me even though I had no connection to the King of the Unicorns death, that I was aware of anyway, but, it wouldn't be the first time I'd been kept out of the loop.

This time Marcus actually loses his footing, but I won't be tempted, not yet, not ever, not by him.

Until I know the whole story I'm on the defensive, once I know how to defeat him in his perfected realm, then I'll take him down.

All at once I get one of Myrelle's crazy ideas, and unlike what Myrelle would've done I contemplate it before actually doing something.

I'm pulled back into Myrelle's spirit aura; she just came to the same conclusion I did.

'If we judge by coincidental link then I'd say he's in such bad physical shape because he's using most of his strength on this magical illusion.

That also means he has a very strong link to the magical foundations of Angels and his gifts will also revolve around a magical centre.'

As soon as we think that, the illusion is shattered and we're once again at the same clearing, in the same positions as before.

A snarl distorted Marcus' face once he realized we'd broken his illusion. What's more, his pupils had dilated so that only a sliver of his forest green eyes was visible around the edge, the rest was covered with his pupil,

'just like a frightened animal...'

a voice warned me.

And as my eyes readjusted to the horrific scene hidden so perfectly around the edges of the clearing Myrelle screamed as the Predators materialized from the shadowed edges of the clearing, prowling toward us.

"It was you then..." I realize with shock that it had been Marcus who brought about the downfall of my kingdom.

The cruel smile that twisted his face gave me my answer. "You killed my parents... You tried to kill my sisters... You ruined my family's life!"

Just as I yell that the sun spirits freeze time and surround me in a surreal yellow glow until I look like a mini version of the sun. The sun spirits appear before me, taking the form of my diseased father.

"You are ready. Your true test has just begun, you've but answered the first question. Never give up, be true to yourself, and trust in your heart. I'll be waiting for you, my only son..."

He faded away, just as the sun hits the horizon, beaconing a new day

I turn my attention back to the fight.

~

'He doesn't know..?'

I could tell he didn't sense a difference, but I had and I could prove it by just looking at his aura.

His choice of his family over himself had enhanced and increased the amount of gold and silver that flecked the frame of his aura.

He was being redeemed, and he didn't even realize it.

I guess if he did I suppose it wouldn't work, huh?

So that's what I noticed when he grew protective of his sisters...

It wasn't just brotherly protection, but he was redeeming himself, he was recreating himself in the image of a pure angel.

I could go on and on describing the different aspects, but I'm pretty sure you get the picture.

The only problem was, no one had ever succeeded in revitalizing their Purity fully, without some side effect or negative impact on another angel.

'I hope you know what you're doing...'

I question the sun spirit's motives quietly before being pulled back to the present by a searing pain in my arm.

Sure enough, one of the predators had managed to creep up on me and sink its teeth into my left arm.

'Must be some kind of neurotoxin in those teeth.' I think, now fully focused on the battle going on around me.

They'd already managed to encircle us but they hadn't separated us, which seemed to be their next goal.

They didn't achieve it though.

Rick dodged left and right, he vaulted over their heads, landing right next to me, totally offensive, but still trying to defend me.

What surprised me most, though, was his expression, which depicted legitimate concern.

He didn't falter though, nor did his attention waver as mine had. He was totally focused on the task at hand.

~

Warding off those Predators proved harder than we first thought. They were faster and smarter than normal hybrids and they were bred to kill.

I felt a shift in the atmosphere and the predators backed off as if they'd been stung and that's when I first noticed the bite mark on Myrelle's arm.

It was a deep wound, four precise punctures that penetrated the skin easily.

The problem was, her arm was dripping blood now. Her flow of blood had, apparently, just then noticed the wounds to her physical body. I can sense Myrelle sending me a thought wave.

'It bit me a while ago, I think its poison is some kind of neurotoxin...'

'So why'd they back off when she started to bleed?'

Then it dawned on me...

Blue Blood has some kind of repellent in it, to ward off evil spirits.

Her blue blood was warding off the Predators.

'And mine will too.'

I take out my hunting knife and carve a groove in my left arm. My blood starts to gush onto the ground, and the Predators back off further, some starting to whimper quietly.

Meanwhile Myrelle is just gaping at me in horror, until a flicker of realization lights her eyes.

Before I could object she took the knife from my hand and carved an added groove in her own arm.

An idea springs to our minds and we cross our arms so that our blood runs to the ground as a single line.

The atmosphere shifts and a taint seems to be removed from our hands that we hadn't even realized was there.

Back at the palace Myrelle's parents notice the shift as well

and all fear leaves them as they look to the west, in the direction of the former golden kingdom. They silently forgive and ask to be forgiven.

The sun shines a little brighter and a sudden burst of song draws the King's and Queen's attention to a nearby peach tree, and on one of the branches sit six goldfinches. Once they notice that they've been seen they seem to swim in the eyes of the King and Queen before disappearing one at a time.

Tears filled the Royal couple's eyes as they lowered their defences completely for the first time in many years, releasing the restraints keeping their children in line.

I'd never felt such freedom as I did when that vow was formally erased.

It was like flying high above the clouds while able to breathe as though I were still on the ground. My spirit soared sky high and I myself felt weightless, as if I was being held in a timeless drifting flow.

Of course that illusion had to be shattered sooner or later but it was nice while it lasted.

We came crashing back down to reality and into a magical chaos.

Marcus was blinded by rage at his failed backup plan and was lashing out at everything in anger and frustration. When he cooled down enough to notice us again his animalistic eyes replaced his usual ones and he wrapped Myrelle in a web of painful enchantments.

"Why do they always target you?" I ask her exasperatedly.

I gain an amused emotion crossed with pain in response.

Magic was costly, both mentally and physically, and still he kept hurting her.

After a while he just gave up on that and went back to tactical, physical assaults while holding her in the air like a ragdoll by a magical thread.

I wished he'd targeted me instead. I would've swapped places with her if I had the choice, but he held me in a locked magical barrier. All I could do was keep fighting and try to ignore her pain. When I opened our link all I found was an immense amount of black pain and a small pinprick of white hope still flickering in the storm.

'What could be so strong that she hasn't given up?' I think, amazed.

It's not like I want her to give up but that memory had to be pretty important if it fuelled her resolve for that long.

I was pulled into another flashback, but this time I'd been the one to trigger it.

I was back at that place Melody's magic had brought before

Myrelle and I had gotten our next powers, at the sand dunes only an hours flight from the sea.

'This is where we first kissed...' I realize.

So this is what she's clinging to...

Physical and magical pain are extremely similar but their effects can e quite different.

Once Marcus realized his magical assaults wouldn't break her, he set about targeting her with physically induced pain. After a while he got that spark of an idea in his eye again and started targeting her wings.

After the first few futile attempts something gave out and he managed to break through her protective defences.

Once he did, he immediately targeted her weakened wing, and broke it.

After the first few seconds of pain and screaming she fainted, unable to cope with the extent of her injuries, but when he broke her wing something inside me snapped and any magical barriers disappeared from around me.

I'd found my twin power, and I was mad, no, scratch that, I was bloody infuriated.

A blast of pure energy sent Marcus crashing into a tree, which caused him to lose his grip on the spell binding Myrelle. Once I'd collected her I sent another shockwave in Marcus's direction and heard him slump against a tree.

Once we'd safely returned to the castle I finally allowed myself to relax a bit, and was joined by Misty and Rose on a bench outside.

"Are you finally done with those major battles now?"

Rose pips into the silence, and I can see Misty's lips already curving into that knowing half smile of hers.

"In my life, there'll always be something to do."

I smile at her and then shift my gaze to Myrelle's window wondering what our next adventure was going to be like, because there was going to be another one.

No-one could stop it, and no-one denied it either.

So… what was next..?

Well, we'd find out soon enough.

Crooked Halo: Extra Chapter

Book 2: Torn Feathers

Teaser

CHAPTER 31: MYRELLE - SHIFTED PERSPECTIVES

Seasons pass me in a blur. The nostalgic summer scent gives way to the moaning song of an autumn breeze accompanying the fiery leaves on their journey through the forests.

Once the wind dies down the weather cools and the first snowflakes fall across the kingdom. Flowers encased in frost turn the world as we know it into a surreal place of unearthly beauty where every surface is dusted in a coating of cold white sparkles that no image, nor artist could ever hope to capture. Later in the year the days find heat once again, and the white blanket that used to cover the world melts away, to shine as dewdrops that cover the garden and sparkle with dawn's first rays.

Rick's still looking for a way to find and free his older sister Silvia, I'm not even sure that the place she exists in is somewhere we can get access to, but his newest findings show that there is a way to create a passage to the semi-dimension where we usually find ourselves when we're in the throngs of a vision, which is what Silvia described her current "home" as.

So we're heading to the Golden Kingdom to see if we can

establish a connection with Silvia's past spirit to help guide the passage to her present location. The problem with the Spirit Passage is that it takes up a lot of magical energy to keep it open, and I can't let it close while Rick's in there, since we don't know if he could find his way back out if I have to reopen it.

The Spirit Passage is basically a portal to another dimension, but you're the one who has to move through it; it's not like some hyper drive you could use on a space ship—just push a button, use some energy, and your there.

You literally have to transcend the distance from our dimension to that one by physical motion, hence the name Spirit Passage.

Because you have to move quite a bit to get there,

at least that's what we think...

Neither of us has been able to actually reach the semi-dimension, and Rick hasn't been able to even open the passage,

so Melody and I keep it open while Rick keeps looking.

It's been about two years since we first met, Rose would be 15 now... I haven't seen her in ages, and neither has Rick.

Rose is staying at the Angel Haven Palace. It was even arranged that she be tutored in the arts of a Princess.

She was completely opposed to the idea of having to learn about stuff she thought was "a complete waste of time."

She wanted to spend her time learning more about the things she wanted to; study music, enjoy the outdoors, go live with her common parents.

It wasn't an option.

Especially considering the fact that her real mother was still alive, though her whereabouts are unknown.

The only reason she ever came around to the idea was because her tutor was Fidel, my older brother.

From what I'd heard though, she wasn't even allowed outside the Palace walls without an escort.

It must be pretty bad then...

Having a new Royal discovered usually meant that the subjects of the kingdom would want to manipulate that figure to get what they wanted, and some were even desperate enough to attack or steal from the Royals should they appear outside the Palace Walls unaccompanied.

Rose wasn't aware of any of this, it meant that she was safest if she was cut off from the outside world for as long as possible,

and, knowing her, she was going to hate it.

We still see Misty from time to time though she wanders about as she pleases. If something interesting happens, you'll usually find her there. She's taken to appearing like a normal angel now though, dropping the act of being a ghost simply because she felt like it.

I manage to hold the Spirit Passage a while longer now.

'Looks like my magical ability has grown stronger', I think to myself, rather pleased.

'Don't be so narrow minded.' came Melody's intrusion, her voice stiff.

'Don't worry, I'll make sure my physical abilities don't diminish.' I reassure her, but on this topic she's rather fussy.

'Aim to increase your physical ability, don't focus too much on magic, stay open minded and balanced in the way that you divide your attention between your:

Heart,

Mind,

Spiritual Connection,

Magical Powers,

And,

Physical Strength and Endeavours.'

She's awfully specific, but I can understand why considering she lost her father to his unbalanced methods of obtaining power.

"I'll keep it in mind." I smile, it fades as my power continues to be drawn out by the Spirit Passage, but returns once Rick steps out of it and I can release the magic keeping it open.

I sigh in relief. With my strength no longer leaving me the magic fades and the true effect of its power finally manages to overcome me.

I replenish my strength with something to eat before settling to rest in the cool shade of a maple tree in the Royal Gardens.

The maples leaves are a fiery orange, verging on red. It's autumn at the moment, though I can feel winter's chill already stirring in the late autumn breeze.

A pair of intelligent brown eyes watch us from a fair distance away, but I can sense Sarah's presence from much further away than where she's currently concealing herself. The vibrant autumn hues do a good job of hiding her physical form from sight though; even I couldn't have picked out her hiding place if she hadn't begun moving towards us.

'That's unusual…' I muse in the private confines of my mind.

'You noticed her too, huh?'

I start at Rick's sudden intrusion, but can't keep the smile

from spreading across my face.

'Yeah, it's going to be important if she's come all this way.' I send back and see his expression turn grim in response.

'You haven't had much luck yet, from your expressions.' Sarah immediately picks up on our demeanour and expressions, but her next words almost give me a heart attack.

'You won't be able to find her by simply opening the Passage at the place where her spiritual essence last existed, the connection needs to be established anew; forge an emotional bond, or use a sacrificial method to find her, and that's meant to be the easy part.' Sarah's thoughts shock both of us to the core. Not only is she telling us of a way to save Silvia, she's warned us about a method we'd want to avoid using. A spark of suspicion kindled in my mind, Sarah wasn't the kind to help out without an ulterior motive.

She focuses her eyes on me with such intensity I'm surprised I managed not to flinch at her piercing gaze.

'You are but the helpers of Fate, don't continue to meddle in affairs that are destined for someone else.'

She then adds, more to herself, though we still catch her words,

'I was asked to tell you of ways to strengthen the connection and have done more than my part, I can only pray for the safety of those dear to you and me now.'

She turns and leaves so swiftly if I'd blinked it would've seemed as though she'd disappeared into thin air.

She left me with an echoing thought, 'Protect those close to your heart, for anything that is negatively inflicted upon them will rebound to harm your very heart.' Though I knew she sent those thoughts to me, I haven't a clue what they're supposed to mean.

~

There was an underlying message in the thought that Sarah sent through to

Myrelle, There's a possibility that something bad could happen to someone close to you, protect them, for if they are injured, you will drown in guilt that accuses you didn't do enough.

What's troubling me is that she sent the message through our link and she also sent me a different warning of sorts.

'Don't meddle in affairs that are destined for someone else,

though each puzzle piece interlinks with another, only one piece is capable of connecting to a certain part of another.'

Judging by the confused expression on Myrelle's features she doesn't understand the warning she was given either.

I myself am at a loss for what the warning means, a puzzle I'm unable to piece together alone. No matter how hard I may try, the pieces won't come together in my head like they're supposed to.

'Find anything new in there this time?' came the gentle intrusion on my thoughts. I smile thinly at Myrelle's concern.

Though it's hard to keep the portal open, it's no walk in the park trying to transcend dimensions either.

It's really tiring to keep walking through a place where there's no way of telling distance nor direction. It's not even a maze,

there are no walls, there's almost nothing here.

It's a wilderness of an endless black sky with the ground only distinguishable by the glowing white mist that swirls around my feet as I move through it. The sky has no sun, moon nor even a single star shining up there.

All I can see in this place is the fog that swallows my feet beneath it and the silvery disk marking the portal itself.

The portal doesn't stay in a fixed position, it flickers and moves according to forces we don't even know, and can't begin to understand.

I have nothing to base my position on.

I don't know which way I'm walking, and my wings confuse me even more. I can't control them at all, a different force isn't controlling them, they just don't react to any commands I give them. It's like they just freeze in the last position they were in when I was last in my dimension.

I haven't told Myrelle about the wings, because I know she'd try to convince me to let her go in there, and though I don't doubt her capabilities, I just don't want to endanger her needlessly.

'That's a rather selfless thought for you to have.'

This time it's Melody who intrudes my thoughts. 'Says the Alacorn who'd give up her life for her friend.' I shoot back, my mood already brightening a bit. The bouts Melody and I have help both of us vent a bit and get into higher spirits if we're feeling down.

'I don't doubt that you'd do the same for someone close to you, if they were in danger.' she argues, and this time I don't reply, because something just dawned on me.

The stirring breeze suddenly picks up, changing to a howling wind that chills me right to the heart.

"Come on, we need to get inside before this gets much worse," Myrelle shouts to be heard over the now howling wind.

We retreat to the Golden Kingdom Castle and reside in one of the less damaged rooms. This room is the only one where the windows hadn't been shattered, and as I do a retake I gasp as I recognize the room.

It was mine.

The room I'd spent the first years of my life in.

Why hadn't it been ravaged like all the other rooms had been?

'Amber? Mind informing me of anything you might know?'

I call my goldfinch and she appears at my side instantly.

Her eyes widen slightly in disbelief as she sees where we are.

'So… The Seal managed to hold then?' she muses, including me in her thoughts.

'What does that mean?' I ask her with as much restraint as I can manage.

'It means that your parents and eldest sister contributed their magical abilities to create a seal for this room to keep out all creatures of darkness and preserve some of the light of the Kingdom.' she states before disappearing again,

I'm glad she spared me the trouble of having to ask her to go.

"What did she tell you?" Myrelle asks, not bothering to hide her exasperation and curiosity.

I don't answer her, my eye catches onto the window latch, a golden brooch the size of a fingernail is embedding in the wood, and inscribed on it are three names.

Rick, Misty, and Rose.

My mind's reeling now.

Maybe Sarah wasn't referring so much towards a to a very specific who when she warned us of the trials to come.

Question was, 'who' exactly was she referring to?

ABOUT THE AUTHOR

Kay was born in the South of Germany and moved to Australia with her family when she was two. She is currently working towards finishing her high school in Sydney. On sunny days she loves rock and tree climbing. Indoors she enjoys a good read and often works on her books when it's cold and wet outside. She loves music, playing the piano and singing in the school choir. She is also undertaking Art as a school subject which she thoroughly enjoys.

www.ingramcontent.com/pod-product-compliance
Lightning Source LLC
Chambersburg PA
CBHW060618130626
46555CB00002B/550